A BERRY CLEVER CORPSE

A.R. WINTERS

❀ Created with Vellum

JOIN THE A.R. WINTERS NEWSLETTER

Find out about the latest releases by AR Winters, and get access to exclusive free copies of her books:

CLICK HERE TO JOIN

You can also follow AR Winters on Facebook

BLURB

Welcome to Sarah's Eatery, where the food is to-die-for!

Kylie's move to Camden Falls didn't go quite as she expected: now she's got two hunky men fighting for her affections, more burnt food than can go on her cafe's Oops Board, and an ex aunt-in-law who won't leave her alone.

And of course there's the latest murder Kylie gets drawn into…

When local real estate bigshot "Mean Mike" Pratt is found dead in his office, accusations fly from every other store-front—in no small part because he owns them!

Kylie's hairdresser, Susie, is dragged into the accusation game as one of the many business owners whose shops were owned by Mike. He and Susie were spotted squabbling in the street over rent negotiations, and word travels fast in little Camden Falls...

Did Susie really kill Mean Mike? Did Susie's boyfriend, trying to protect his girl from Mike's predatory practices, have something to do with it? Or maybe it was the hip coffee shop owner, or even Susie's rival beauty salon owner? And why is Mike's neighbor Tina, behaving so strangely?

While she learns the secrets of baking, Kylie, with help from her best friend Zoey, searches high and low to learn the secrets of who really killed Mean Mike!

CHAPTER 1

"It's going to cost how much?"

Barely a month ago, I, Kylie Berry, became the brand new owner of an entire city block thanks to my cousin Sarah. She fell in love and moved away from the tiny southeastern Kentucky town that I now called home, but before she went, she sold me her café—and everything attached to it—for nothing down, which was good because I'd had nothing to put down. I'd been destitute and homeless up to five seconds prior.

While no longer homeless, I was still destitute and standing in the sub-basement of my newly acquired building.

Before this morning, I hadn't even known that my building had a sub-basement.

Standing next to me was Lou Sizemore, a local plumber. Only he wasn't *a* local plumber, he was *the* local plumber, as in *the* best, *the* guru, and *the* most expensive. I'd been lucky to get him to come out on a Saturday morning. Together, we were staring up at and around the side of something that put me in mind of a train locomotive. It was huge and complex, and if open on both ends, it was big enough to drive a car through.

"Your boiler's busted. You'll need a new one," Lou said. He was middle-aged, close to six feet, and had a round beer belly. He was wearing a button-up shirt tucked into jeans held up with suspenders and a John Deere baseball cap that he adjusted by lifting its front rim and then pulling it back down. "It's an explosion hazard. It's got to be replaced. Can't be used 'til then."

"Are you sure it'll cost that much?" He'd quoted a price that had left me feeling faint. I really needed to sit down.

The quote was enough to buy a high-end minivan.

He shrugged, clearly not affected by my soaring anxiety. "Labor, parts, and transport, not to mention the removal and transport of your current system."

But he *had* just mentioned it. I had no idea how he was going to get the old one out of the building and the new one in, but I wasn't going to ask. At least not right now, maybe later. When I was calmer. When I had a pound of chocolate sitting next to me and a large glass of merlot in my hand.

"What if I didn't replace it right away and we just shut the current system down and went without for a little while?"

He looked at me like I'd asked if my farts smelled like candy canes. "You lose heating for the entire building, have no hot water, and your pipes will be at risk for freezing. If they freeze, they might burst. If they burst, they'll flood your sub-basement and parts of the rest of the building. That'll lead to mold, property damage, unsanitary conditions and the possible evacuation and quarantine of the entire building."

I gulped. "Right. So... payment plans. Do you offer them?" If he said no, I was toast. Burnt toast. Charred and bitter and good for nothing. The one part of the building that I had anything directly to do with was the café, but it was still operating in the red—deep in the red. Largely because I was the chef... a terrible, awful, horrible chef. People had hypothetically died because of my cooking. Hypothetically as in never proven.

Like I said, the café was a long way from turning a profit. I'd been keeping it afloat and operational with the help of the income from the rest of the building's renters. Paying off the price Lou had quoted would require every spare penny from the building's income for the next six month. If one of the storefronts that rented from me decided to pull out or wasn't able to pay me, I wouldn't be able to pay Lou. Of course, if I didn't replace the boiler, I could get sued for breach of contract or the businesses could decide to go elsewhere.

Lou made a grumbling noise that I couldn't discern the meaning of, then he shrugged, picked up the front of his cap, scratched his scalp through his thinning hair, and pulled his cap back down. "I liked Sarah. She was a good woman." I considered mentioning she wasn't dead, only getting married, but I kept my mouth shut. Lou continued talking. "We can probably work something out." He pulled out a business card. "Call my office. We'll get you taken care of."

I took his card with a shaking hand. "Any idea of the time frame before things are up and running again?"

His eyes scanned the monstrous contraption before us. "Should be able to get 'er done within a couple of weeks."

I tried to remember what the weather reports had said. A cold snap was heading our way. "Can we at least leave this one running until we get the new one installed?"

He looked from me to the boiler then

back again. "If you're okay with the chance of it exploding, ripping through half your building and possibly killing some people in the process."

"So… that's a maybe."

He turned around and walked away, mumbling, "I miss Sarah."

Definitely not a fan of me or my sense of humor.

~

I walked in the front door of my café, *Sarah's Eatery,* five minutes later. Zoey, Joel, Jack, and Agatha were all sitting at the counter in front of the café's grill while Brad stood behind the counter and served coffee that he had undoubtedly made himself.

"You finally got the good stuff in," he said. "Had to grind it myself, but that's a good thing."

Brad didn't work for me, at least not in the sense that I paid him. He was a civil servant. You know, the kind who carried a badge, a gun, and had the power to haul my tushie into jail if I did something wrong. He was an officer with the Kentucky State Police, and had the sexy, muscle-hugging uniform to prove it.

Zoey took a sip, and her perfectly manicured brows went up in surprise. "Wow, this is good." Her honeyed skin had a natural glow, and her almond-shaped eyes sported a warrior princess look today with eyeliner that was ready to pick up a sword and shield. Her hair was jet black, thick and wild, and her timeless Asian beauty could shift her from looking like a twelve year old one minute to a worldly thirty year old the next. In truth, she was twenty-two with a lot of life miles under her belt. She and I had trekked a few of those miles together. She had my back when the rest of the town was calling me a murderer, and then I did the same for her. Throw in a few near death experiences and you had a pretty complete history of our dynamic duo routine.

Joel stood up while still tightening the lid on his thermos, all six foot five inches of him. He had the body of Paul Bunyan and the heart of a herald, and he put his natural talents to work as the chief editor, owner and reporter of the Camden Falls Herald, one of the town's two local newspapers. "Mind if I head out the back way? Shorter walk in all this cold."

"Sure. No problem," I said, waving him off while wishing for the opportunity to say more. Joel had recently shown up to take me out on a date, but a gun-wielding psychopath had been a bit of a mood killer. Joel sadly hadn't made any efforts to reschedule our outing, and I was worried that people's repeated desire to kill me had put him off the idea of taking me on a nice date. But with the repeated attempts on my life, I could really use a fun evening out.

"Speaking of the cold, dear," Agatha said while holding her cup of hot coffee in both hands as if for the warmth that it could give her, "it's feeling nippy in here." The spry eighty-two-year-old's elegant shoulders were draped in a stunning shawl that she had no doubt knitted with her own two hands. Her silver-haired pixie cut, dangly earrings, and cascading bracelets were all for style and did nothing for warmth. Neither did her flowing, gossamer style of dress.

That she was cold in the place I was trying to make a home away from home hurt my heart like little else had.

"I'm sorry, Agatha. There's a problem with the building's boiler, but let me get a fire going in the fireplace."

Yep, the café had a fireplace. I'd thought it odd the first time I'd seen it, and I'd never gotten the chance to ask my cousin Sarah about it, but I was thankful for it now. The fireplace plus some over-stuffed chairs made up what I liked to call the cozy corner, and it was where the knitting club, book club and other groups tended to congregate when they came in. And I was sure that they stayed longer because of the little corner's warm, welcoming feel.

"That's all right, sweetheart. I saw Sage napping back there. I'll fix up the fire and she can be my lap warmer."

Agatha smiled and it healed the hurt in my heart. If Agatha was happy, then I was happy.

"I'll bring you a snack in a little bit," I told her as she strolled away with that characteristic dancer's grace.

"Did Lou take care of you? Told you he'd take care of you," Brad said. "What was the verdict?"

"I need a new boiler."

"Ouch," Brad said with a wince. He twisted on the top of his thermos. "I heard that a cold snap is moving in. You gonna have heat in that upstairs apartment of yours?"

"Yeah, sure. Of course I will." Lies, lies, lies. When would I ever stop lying? The only other heat I had besides what the boiler provided was the oven. I supposed I could always drag my mattress from my bedroom into the kitchen. Lying it on one room's floor was as good as lying it on another.

Brad didn't look convinced. "You've got my number," he said, then kissed me on the cheek as he headed out the café's front door. Brad had also made a date with me that he hadn't kept. Pesky dead bodies showing up always seemed to interest him more than me.

That left Zoey and Jack, but it was Jack who I wanted to talk to. He had the cool, regal bearing of a younger—and bald—Morgan Freeman. His dark skin had red and gold undertones, his eyes twinkled like embering coals, and he had a bit of a Mona Lisa smile. I always had the sense that he was amused, but I could never tell if he was amused with me… or at me. I really hoped that it was the former. Jack owned a bank, and, well, a loan was sounding really good right about now.

"Ladies," Jack said in salutations of his impending parting. Standing up, he slid on his full-length camel hair coat and then simultaneously put on and tipped his fedora hat. "Good coffee, Kylie."

"Thanks!" I went pigeon-toed and played with my hands like a nervous schoolgirl at his compliment. Jack was very adult, and even at twenty-nine I wasn't sure I'd gotten there. Being around him made me feel like a kid struggling to get a clue about life, and Jack seemed to have everything already figured out.

I watched him walk out with the words "I need a favor" on the tip of my tongue the whole time. But the moment wasn't right. Asking a person for money was never easy—at least it wasn't for me. I'd never been in this situation before, but my ex-husband had left me with nothing when we divorced by way of an absurd prenup that I never should have signed.

With Jack out the door, that left me and Zoey.

"I've got a client call scheduled in half an hour. Mind if I make a sandwich to go?" Zoey was a tech genius, and she worked doing independent tech support for the rest of us who were less knowledgeable. That is to say, everyone.

"Sure! Go for it." She made better sandwiches than me, anyway.

Zoey headed to the back kitchen, and I went behind the counter to see if I could figure out what Brad did to make the coffee so good. While I was staring into a canister of whole beans, wondering if they needed to be blended into a fine powder or only cut into rough chunks, the bell on the café's front door chimed.

I looked up to find Susie walking in. Susie owned a hair salon and had recently given me to-die-for highlights and a cut. She was nine years older than me, the same age as my ex, and was also my ex's ex. They'd been high school sweethearts. She'd dumped him right after he slept with the whole cheerleading squad and two of his teachers. Sadly, not much had changed between when she and Dan had been together and when he and I had been married. The man savored his variety.

"It's Friday!" Susie said with a cheery smile. But I wasn't buying it. It was a false cheer, and I instantly knew something was wrong. Her face was doing all the things that it was supposed to do to show happiness, but all I saw was distraught sadness.

Smiling with mechanical perfection,

she wiggled her large, metallic to-go cup in the air. Friday was my new free-fills day for anyone who managed to make it in Monday through Thursday. So far, Susie was my only customer to do it besides my longtime regulars.

"Hey, what's up? You okay?" I couldn't keep the worry from my voice and didn't even try. I took her to-go cup from her and filled it with the last of the coffee that Brad had made. It was just enough to fill her cup to two-thirds, but I knew she'd top it off with lots of cream and sugar. I'd started buying organic cream just for her. Since my cooking was terrible, I used every other opportunity I could to make my customers happy.

I handed the coffee cup back over to her and then set out the cream and sugar so that she could top it off herself. Watching her finish it off was like watching a ritual, and I could see how it soothed her.

Susie shook her head. Her smile was gone, and she was no longer trying to hide her misery. "My landlord is raising the rent on my salon space. He's almost doubling it."

"Doubling it? Can he do that?"

"He sure can. Waltzed into the shop yesterday right in the middle of me doing someone's hair. It was humiliating."

"Sit," I ordered and then grabbed her a cheese Danish. I nuked it for fifteen seconds and then slid it in front of her. She picked at it with her perfectly manicured fingers and ate little nibbles of it. "Now tell me what happened."

"I was in my shop with old lady Cruthers." I didn't know who that was, but didn't say. "Mr. Pratt came waltzing in, shouting at the top of his lungs like he was standing on some stage and needing to be heard by an audience. He told me what my new rent would be and that it would be effective on the first."

"That's three days from now. How can he do that?"

"Well, I told him he couldn't, and that's when he laughed at me. Said he could do anything he wanted, and that it was all in the contract I'd signed. The only reason I rented that space was because the rent was so low. I've only been there six months, I've been on time with everything, and now I'll be paying way more than any other space I'd looked at when deciding where to set up shop." She shook her head. "I don't know what to do. This is going to put me out of business. The overhead will be too high."

"Can't you go somewhere else? Set up shop somewhere else?"

"He said that if I do that, he'll sue for breach of contract and I'll have to pay for his and my lawyer fees on top of the rent for the remaining months. And it's a two-year contract."

I'd never met this Mr. Pratt, but I was hating him. He was sounding more and more like a great big bully.

"What will you do?" I asked. Susie was stuck between a rock and a hard place.

"I could kill him," she said. "That would get me out of the contract."

I was too stunned for words, and I knew that I was wearing my aghast surprise on my face. It took Susie a moment to notice, but when she did, she laughed. "Oh, hun," she said, reaching a hand across to squeeze mine. "It was a bad joke. I'm sorry."

Zoey chose that moment to come out of the kitchen, mammoth-sized sandwich on a plate with chips, covered with plastic wrap. I knew she'd bring the plate back and I wasn't going to charge her for a sandwich she made herself, but she put a twenty on the counter for her coffee and sandwich anyway. A hefty over-payment.

"What's wrong?" Zoey asked, looking between the two of us.

"I'm plotting my landlord's murder," Susie said. "I figured I'd be in good company." She winked at Zoey.

"But we didn't do anything," I said. "We were innocent."

"And that's just what I'll say, too!"

Zoey dug out a chip from under the plastic wrap and crunched down on it. "You gonna disappear the body or leave it out for everyone to find?"

"Hey! Come on you two," I complained. "I can't go through this again. Did you know that some old lady let me cut in front of her at the grocery store? I thought she was just being nice, then she whispered to me that she'd like for me to kill her husband, said she could make it worth my while."

That had Susie's and Zoey's attention.

"What did you say?" Susie asked, her expression rapt.

"I didn't say anything! I just nervously giggled and then pretended she didn't exist. She bumped me with her buggy three times trying to get me to turn back around, but I wouldn't. I refused."

Susie and Zoey broke out laughing, but I was failing to see the humor. I did not appreciate my growing reputation as the murder queen of Camden Falls.

"I don't understand why people keep killing each other. I mean, can't people just learn to get along?"

The front door of my café burst open and the Wicked Witch of the West flew in on her broom. Yes, she had an actual broom today. Her sudden appearance was the universe's way of trying to make me take back my words—that I couldn't understand why people kept killing each other—but I refused to do it. The universe could suck it. No backsies.

"Hey, Aunt—I mean, uh… Dorothy, where'd you get that?" She was my ex-aunt-in-law. Unlike my ex-husband, I hadn't been able to shed her from my life after the divorce. In fact, her hatred of me had amplified to the gleeful hate of a zealot.

In her hand was a short decorative broom, the type you'd hang on a wall. It was made of twigs with a rich red-brown bark that had been tied together with twine, and it was heavily scented with cinnamon. It smelled really nice.

Ex-Aunt Dorothy waved the broom, sending perfumed air wafting over me, and barked her commandment of the day. "Stay away from him, you harlot!"

"Stay away from who?" How could she have known about my non-date with Brad? Or, was it my non-date with Joel that had her upset?

Bruce and Maryann Hibbert, my ex's

parents, burst through the door behind Dorothy and flanked her. "Isn't it such good news?" Maryann asked as she did her best to wrangle the broom out of Dorothy's hand. "Have you heard?"

"Heard what?" My heart was afraid to beat. Bruce and Maryann had quickly become the harbingers of doom since I'd moved to town, and they always delivered their terrible news with huge, toothy smiles on their faces. The worst was that they weren't even malicious smiles. They were genuinely the happy, enthusiastic smiles of people who had never given me any reason to doubt that they cared about me.

"Dan's going to be in town!" Bruce said.

"And he'd sure love to see his gal," Maryann added with a conspiratorial grin.

Dan was my ex. I suddenly wondered if we could make Mr. Pratt's grave a double grave and add Dan's body to it. I could see the three of us—Susie, Zoey and me—out in the woods in the middle of the night, digging a hole, nice and deep. I hadn't moved halfway across the country to be troubled with a man who had done his best to ruin me. I'd been left with nothing in the divorce, and then he'd destroyed my reputation and had made me un-hirable. If it hadn't been for my cousin Sarah, I had no doubt that I would still be dependent on the kindness of others for the bare basics of survival.

"Bruce, Maryann, I love you guys, but Dan and me are done. I'm with Aun—I mean, I'm with Dorothy on this one. I'm going to stay away from him. I adore you guys, but… he was not good to me."

The joy in Bruce and Maryann's expressions fell away, leaving their faces long and forlorn, but the self-righteous, malicious glee in Dorothy's expression grew. I was tempted to say that I'd have dinner with them and Dan just to spite her, but stopped short of promising to do something akin to emotional suicide.

"I'll make your favorite just in case you change your mind," Maryann said. "Pot roast with extra onions."

That was Dan's favorite. It had always been his favorite. But through the years, his parents had attached everything they knew about Dan to me as if we were one person with one personality. "That's very sweet of you, Maryann. Thank you."

With each taking an arm, Dan's parents marched Dorothy out of the café, and I laid my forehead on the counter.

"You know," Susie said with a twinkle in her eye, "there was one thing that Dan was awfully good at. A visit might not be such a bad idea."

My head snapped up. "Not you too. Out. Out… Go on with you. I'll be sure to send Dan your way if he starts sniffing around."

Susie got up and headed for the door. "Don't you dare," she laughed. "My sweetie's heard the stories about us from high school. Dan shows up and you'll have me in all kinds of trouble. He's all yours." With a wink, she was out the door, not giving me a chance for a snappy comeback of my own.

"Think he's flying or driving in from

Chicago?" Zoey asked. "If he's flying, I can put on the no-fly list, get him arrested with a cavity search."

"I love you." Once again, Zoey had proven herself to be the best friend ever.

CHAPTER 2

I tried not to yawn as Brenda and I stood bent over, studying the cake I'd just finished baking. It was a mocha chocolate bundt cake sprinkled with a light dusting of powdered sugar. It looked amazing, but it had three siblings sitting next to it that hadn't fared as well. One had turned to crumbs, one had the consistency of rubber, and the third was incredibly dense and somehow managed to weigh three times the others.

Looking at the cake that had turned out well, I felt incredibly proud. The sense of accomplishment was enormous. It was right up there with achieving world peace. For the cake's mocha component, I'd even used the fancy new coffee Brad had gotten me to order. I'd almost put the coffee's ground, raw beans into the batter, but thankfully Brenda had stopped me and explained that the coffee had to be brewed first.

Brenda was my morning angel, and I'd inherited her from my cousin Sarah. She was short with jet black hair that fell past her shoulders, and was soft in a very grandmotherly, huggable way. She'd never been anything but kind to me, and I adored her. I'd been in the kitchen since five AM trying to make the perfect cake, and she'd been right here with me since five-thirty. It was now ten-thirty.

"That looks gorgeous, darlin'," she said with a pat on my shoulder. She groaned and stretched as she straightened up. "You're comin' along. Making real progress with your skills."

"Thanks, Brenda." Her words of praise would keep me happy for the next two hours at least. "What do you think I should do with the others?"

"What do you plan to do with this one?" she asked, pointing to the one cake that had turned out well.

"Susie's having some trouble with her landlord, and I was going to go talk to him and see if I could smooth things out." That was only the iceberg's tip of the truth. What I actually planned to do was go over to Mr. Pratt's office with Zoey and blackmail him into sticking with the terms of Susie's original contract. Zoey had spent Saturday and Sunday using her ninja-like computer skills to dig up some juicy dirt on Mr. Pratt. Turns out that Mr. Pratt had done a few things that the IRS would be very interested to learn about.

The cake was a token gift to try to take the edge off the message. I would prefer not to make an outright enemy of Mr. Pratt. My ex-Aunt Dorothy did a very nice job of filling my enemy quota all on her own.

"You could take the other cakes to the local food pantry or take 'em over to the homeless shelter. Some of the folks there might have teeth good enough to handle gnawin' their way through them cakes."

Homeless shelter... That struck a nerve. Things had been so dire for me prior to leaving Chicago that I'd been living in a women's shelter. Donating the cakes to the local homeless shelter sounded both like a great idea and a cruel one. I hoped they would forgive my terrible first attempts at making the cake!

Brenda headed on her way to do grandmotherly things and my full wait staff—college students Melanie and Sam—made it in. Zoey showed up soon after, and with a Brenda-made lasagna and a simple tossed salad available to serve to customers, I left the café in Melanie and Sam's capable hands and Zoey and I loaded up her car with all four cakes and headed out.

"Think Susie will get mad if we interfere?" I asked Zoey once we were on our way.

"If we save her from getting jacked around by her landlord, I think she'll throw us a party."

I thought about my own situation and the looming cost of replacing the boiler. True to his word, Lou Sizemore's office had drafted a payment plan. I'd be able to pay the amount due each month, but it would leave almost nothing extra. The café was still not operating in the black, and I was going to run out of money to cover operating costs if I didn't turn its cash flow around.

If I closed the café, that would mean I'd have to fire Melanie and Sam. It would also mean losing the connection with the community that I was slowly building. I hadn't realized it while I was married, but Dan had purposely isolated me from both family and friends so that when we'd gotten divorced, I'd been left with no one. My whole life had been him and the business we'd built together. Now, without him, I was finally at a place in my life where I had people outside of family who mattered to me—and I mattered to them, too. If I lost the café, I was sure that I'd lose the community of friendship that I was on my way to building. I'd be alone again… and I didn't want to be alone. Not like that.

Raising rent on my building's storefronts had crossed my mind. It had crossed it about thirty thousand times over the weekend. I wouldn't be able to do it right away, but a couple of shops had leases that would soon be up for renewal. But then I thought about Susie and how much she was struggling to make it, and I thought about Mr. Pratt's willingness to gouge her for every dime he could squeeze out of her. I didn't want to be a Mr. Pratt, and I didn't want the community to see me that way. I would probably raise the rent on the leases scheduled for renewal, but the increases would be based on fair business practices. What those fair businesses practices would be, I didn't have a clue. It was yet another thing to ask Jack, the bank owner, about.

Zoey pulled up in front of Mr. Pratt's house fifteen minutes later. He'd converted his garage to a home office, and I'd been told that was where he did all of his business. The neighborhood was nice, and his house was at the end of a cul-de-sac. There were tall, mature trees all around, and his house was bordered by a small park.

"You want to do the blackmailing or should I?" Zoey asked. Her eyeliner had taken a turn from Viking warrior princess toward Marilyn Manson. She was wearing black lace-up hiker boots that had been jacked up with four-inch platform soles with a loose-fitting dress made snug with a very wide wrap-around cloth belt. The dress itself had a slit up both thighs and showed off her fishnet stockings. She hadn't bothered with a coat.

In contrast I was wearing jeans and a plain, tucked-in T under a red, three-quarter length coat, and I was pretty sure I still had some smudges of chocolate on my T.

"I'm thinking that the news of his impending blackmail might be taken more seriously if it came from you," I said.

"Cool." Her full lips quirked into a crooked smile. "Blackmailing someone is on my bucket list anyway."

Win-win. I liked those.

We got out of her car, and I retrieve the one good cake from the back seat. Then we started up the gently inclined driveway that led to his garage office door.

"You don't wanna do that."

We stopped and looked around for the owner of the voice. I didn't see anyone at first, but then Zoey pointed in the direction of the park. There was a huge oak tree right at the edge of Mike's property where the park began. Underneath it stood a man.

"What?" I asked, unsure of what I'd heard.

"You don't wanna do that. You don't wanna go in there," the man said. He had the body of a skeleton with skin stretched over it. His cheekbones were sharp, and his skin had a slightly pale yellow pallor. He was dressed in what looked like army surplus clothes that hung from his skinny frame.

"Why not?" I asked.

Then I heard the sirens. Lots of sirens. And they were coming our way.

CHAPTER 3

Zoey and I stood at the edge of the parking lot with our new four best friends, Derek, Winnie, Patty, and Manny. Derek had been the man who had warned us against going in Mean Mike's office. That's what Derek, Patty, Winnie, and Manny called Mr. Pratt—Mean Mike. I guessed the name said it all. Except I was a little confused because they all seemed to use his name fondly.

Together, we watched a covered body bag get rolled out of Mr. Pratt's office. Inside of it rested Mean Mike himself.

"He had one of them big shredders," Winnie said, holding her arms three feet apart and then waving her hand four feet in the air. She was somewhere in her 30s to 50s, though I couldn't tell where exactly. Her face was weathered with deep lines feathering off from her lips, but her hands were as pretty and smooth as a hand model's. Her eyes had a slightly rheumy look, though. She looked as though she had grabbed life with both hands to ride it hard and had gotten a bit used up in the process. "He was always shredding. No loose scraps of paper in his whole office. Everything, he'd shred."

Patty sniffed back some tears. "I told him not to be wearing that long scarf of his while he shredded. Never would listen."

"What happened? Do you know?" I asked.

"It was me who found him," Derek said. "Cold is coming, and Mean Mike said he'd have us some of them silvery survival blankets, the ones that look like tin foil, and some duct tape so that we could weatherproof our house." He pointed his thumb over his shoulder to indicate the direction of his "house."

I twisted around to see it. It was a standalone cinderblock public bathroom with his and hers sides. The roof was lifted several inches above the cinderblock walls, allowing air to freely flow in and out of the structure.

"How do you stay warm in there?" I asked, and was answered by Patty's sneeze.

"It ain't easy," she said. She was bundled in what looked like a surplus wool blanket. Her nose was red and raw from a cold it looked like she'd been fighting for a while.

These people were homeless, in the middle of winter, and their benefactor had just been wheeled away in an ambulance that didn't bother to use its sirens as it left. There was no longer any hurry. The emergency was passed because the person in jeopardy was dead.

"How'd he die?" I asked Derek.

"The shredder got 'em. That fancy scarf of his was wrapped around his neck and both ends of it was pulled into the shredder. When I went in his office, the shredder was making all kinds of noise and it was laying on top of Mean Mike. His face was shoved right up against the mouth of the thing."

"Was he breathing?" Zoey asked.

"Naw, he was gone. Been gone. He was blue, his eyes bugged out and bleeding, and his tongue was swollen and sticking out," Derek said.

"His eyes were bleeding?" I tried not to shiver at the image.

"Not *bleeding* bleeding," Derek said. "Like, bleeding inside. Red spots. The man was gone. I used his phone to call 911 then left. Didn't touch nothin'."

I kept thinking about the blankets Mr. Pratt had promised them and the more intense cold that was on its way.

"Why do you call him 'Mean Mike?'" Zoey asked.

"Cause he was always yellin'," Winnie said. "I didn't think he'd die this way. I thought he'd have himself a stroke. He'd get so mad. We could hear him all the way out here."

"Did you hear him today?" I asked.

"Not today," Manny said, slurring his words a little.

If they could hear him yelling when he was mad, I wondered why nobody heard him yelling when he was getting strangled. But wrap something tight around my neck and squeeze, I wouldn't be yelling very loudly either. "Who would he yell at?"

Derek shrugged. "Anybody. Everybody. Himself."

"He never yelled at me," Patty said with pride in her voice.

"Me neither," Winnie said. "He never yelled at us, but he sure yelled at everyone else."

"Did he yell at anyone today?" Zoey asked.

Derek shrugged. "Kinda like asking if the wind blowed. Of course it blowed."

"Did you see anyone come to his office today?" I asked.

Nobody answered right away. They all looked at each other or somewhere else entirely.

"We don't know nothin'," Derek said. "We're just trying to live our lives."

It was clear: if they did know something, they weren't telling. Did that mean that they were protecting someone? Or was it that they didn't want to get involved? But Derek had already gotten involved. He'd called 911. It was an action that had the police interviewing him for forty-five minutes. The whole time they had talked to him, he looked as though he'd wanted to crawl out of his skin and slither away, leaving an empty husk for the police to question.

"You guys want a ride to the shelter?" Zoey asked. "Like you said, it's due to turn extra cold."

"No," Patty said curtly and then sneezed. It was a wet and disturbing sound, but not half as disturbing as the chest echoing cough that followed. I resisted the urge to take a step away. Barely.

"What's wrong with going to the shelter?" Zoey pushed.

The group looked at each other and

then Derek, their habitual spokesman, spoke up. "Cory Gardener. He keeps threatening to kill Manny in his sleep, and he pushed Patty into the wall when nobody weren't looking."

I knew Zoey and I couldn't stay, but walking away didn't feel right either. These people had so little, yet their need was so great. And they hadn't asked us for anything.

"I've got cakes," I blurted, and then handed over the best one, the one that had been meant for Mr. Pratt. Patty took it and cradled it in her arms. She smiled big once she had the edge of the covering tin foil pulled up far enough to see what was beneath. She pinched a piece off and took a nibble, and her smile got even bigger.

I couldn't leave these people here this way. I couldn't.

"Do you know where *Sarah's Eatery* is on Main Street?" I asked. Patty nodded and the rest did, too. "I'm the owner."

"You're that lady who killed them two people," Patty said, her eyes big and innocent. "It's okay, though. I heard they needed killin'."

A squeak escaped me. I gulped hard to get my vocals under control. "You're welcome to come stay in the café when the cold sets in." The temperature was due to drop into the single digits in a few days.

"She wants to kill us, too!" Manny exclaimed.

"Hush, now," Winnie chastised him. "If she wanted to kill us, she could poison us with that cake." She looked at me expectantly.

Smiling and feeling awkward, I peeled back the aluminum foil for the edge of the cake farthest away from Patty and her coughing. I pinched off a piece, leaned back my head and dropped it in my mouth.

I froze. Stunned. The cake was good. *Really* good! I'd baked a good cake!

Tears flooded my eyes, but I willed them away.

"See there," Winnie said, elbowing Manny. "She's not trying to kill us. If she wanted us dead, all she'd need to do is wait for the weather to do it for her."

"Be no satisfaction in letting the weather do it for her," Manny countered. "Maybe she likes the thrill of doin' it herself."

"Well you can just stay out here and freeze, old man," Winnie snapped. "I'm gonna go stay at the café." She gave me a toothy smile, and I felt a lot better about walking away and leaving them there.

I felt almost human about it.

When we got in the car, Zoey turned to me. "You sure you know what you're doing? People like that, they come with baggage. Sometimes dangerous baggage."

I nodded, trying to look much more sure of myself than I was. "I'm pretty sure that they saw Mr. Pratt's murderer."

"Why, you seen a mirror around here?"

"No, not them. I don't think it was them."

"And you're sure of that? Sure enough to let them come in and spend the night alone with you?"

"Well, no… There'll be two locked doors between us. I'll be upstairs in my apartment."

"Because that's worked out so well for you in the past."

I was getting frustrated. "They didn't do it!" I fell silent, then asked, "So you think he was murdered too, that it wasn't an accident?"

Zoey pursed her lips and answered resignedly, "Yeah."

"And we're going to figure out who it was?"

Zoey gave me her best lopsided grin, all resignation dropping away. "Yeah."

A tap sounded at the window, and I nearly jumped so hard that I hit my head on the top of the car. It was Derek.

Zoey started the engine to power up the car, and I hit the button to roll down the window. I wondered if I had any money in my purse, and was preparing to reach for it in answer to his impending question, when he stopped me dead in my tracks.

"I seen who did it," Derek said.

"Suze... Susie Q... Susan—something like that. She came running out of Mean Mike's office when I was coming 'round the corner from the park."

"Susie..." I whispered, not meaning to.

"Yeah, yeah. The hair lady. That's her."

CHAPTER 4

Monday evening came and went. Zoey loaned me a space heater to help me stay warm at night, and I suffered through a very, very cold shower.

I didn't see or hear from Susie.

Tuesday rolled in with me up long before dawn. I baked another mocha chocolate bundt cake. Okay, I baked two, but it only took me the two tries to get it right this time. It was a big hit with the customers, and I charged full price. No Oops board for the bundt!

I texted Susie. I called Susie. I drove by Susie's dark and locked up hair salon.

No Susie.

Wednesday morning I served breakfast to Brad with the words burning my throat, "Susie killed him!" But despite what homeless Derek saw, I knew it wasn't true. It couldn't be true. Susie was my friend, not a cold-blooded murderer.

"It was a crime of passion," Brad said as he scarfed down his scrambled eggs. He'd only found one small piece of eggshell to push to the side.

Susie could have done a crime of passion. Anybody could do a crime of passion. That's why they called it a crime of passion. It wasn't crime of premeditated or crime of strategy. No, it was passion. Passion happened within the moment. It was fueled by emotion.

I'd never seen Susie as overwrought. I'd never seen her as anyone but unflappable. She was quick with a joke and a smile, and looked for the bright side of every situation. She didn't seem like a crime of passion type of gal.

In contrast, Mr. Pratt's nickname was Mean Mike. *Mean* Mike. Maybe Mean Mike got a little too mean. Maybe he triggered a rage in Susie that overwhelmed her. Maybe he attacked her and she'd had to defend herself!

"They found fingerprints all over that shredder," Brad said. "Fingerprints that weren't Michael Pratt's, but they're not in the national database either."

Brad was drunk on good coffee and almost-good eggs. He wasn't normally so chatty with the specifics of the murders that happened in town, of course he'd had me at the top of the list for those other murders. I figured that he figured I'd had nothing to do with this one.

"Not in the database? What does that mean?"

"Means the perp's got no priors," Brad said, taking a big bite of toast... or, well, warm bread smeared with butter. It wasn't very toasty.

Susie did it! The words flashed in the frontal lobe of my brain like bright neon. I was sure Brad would be able to see it if he looked at me.

"Have you talked to those homeless people again, the ones that were living in the park next to Mean Mike's—uh, Mike's —house?"

"Mmm, talk to them every day. Seen nothing. Know nothing. Too drunk or high. Unreliable witnesses even if they did know something."

Unreliable!

My brain seized onto that word like a life raft. Susie might not have done it! Derek had said he'd seen Susie there that day, but maybe he'd seen somebody else. Maybe he hadn't seen anyone at all.

"I know I shouldn't be tellin' you this," Brad said, leaning forward conspiratorially and dropping his voice even though the only other person in the café was on the far side against the windows and out of earshot, "but we got your ex's high school sweetheart on the hook for the murder. She lawyered up about two seconds into her questioning, though, so no prints from her yet. When we get 'em, though, I know we'll have a match."

My stomach fell and a flush of fever surged through me. "Susie?"

Brad stopped eating mid-chew. He

swallowed. "You know her?" His tone had changed from conspiratorial to accusatory.

"Well, yeah. She cut and colored my hair."

Brad's turned red and he jabbed at his eggs. Then, he scooped what was left of his eggs onto his toast and folded it in half before getting up off his stool. "Can't tell you nothin'. Always sticking your nose right into the middle of somebody's death. You stay out of this one, Kylie. Stay out of it."

He left in a huff, and I resisted throwing the plate out after him. Tomorrow I was going to put extra shell in his eggs.

The rest of the day ticked by without word from Susie, but Agatha and her knitting club members paid me a visit. They came bearing gifts—or, more precisely, loans. Between the lot of them, they donated sixteen beautiful, hand-knitted afghans of every design imaginable. They were gorgeous. I told them that if any of the ladies wanted to put a for sale tag on their afghans in case any of the customers fell in love with them, I'd be sure to hold onto the proceeds until I saw them again. A couple of the ladies took me up on it. It was the least I could do.

Wednesday ended in a cold whisper that had me wondering if I'd have any customers on Thursday. I moved my floor mattress into the kitchen, turned on the oven on one side of me and put the plug-in, portable radiator that Zoey had loaned me on the other. With Sage sleeping on top of my head, I actually managed to stay toasty.

The shower was again brutal. My teeth chattered for twenty minutes afterward. I couldn't stop trembling. My hair was a disaster and felt coated because I'd spent the bare minimum time possible to wash the shampoo out. Even though I'd recently splurged on buying a towel, I still air dried but I did it sitting right in front of an open oven with the heat cranked up.

That didn't last long, though. Worrying about Sage jumping into it and scorching her tiny paws aged me five years before I shut the thing up. In the end, I opted to simply lean my back against the closed oven door. There, I soaked in the radiant heat until it reached my bones.

Downstairs in the café's kitchen, I gladly spent the day's prep time there cooking. I'd looked up a recipe for hearty winter chili. I was tempted to put in extra cayenne pepper but forced myself to stick to the recipe. Even then I got things wrong, but the end result was still surprisingly yummy.

I decided to serve the chili over baked potatoes. So, I baked a large flat of potatoes, again following a recipe. It was surprisingly hard to find a recipe for simply putting a bunch of potatoes in an oven, and I ended up having to put them back in to cook longer three times before they were done. Only one exploded. I guessed that I'd forgotten to cut it to let it vent.

Out in the dining area, I added the chili and potato to the Oops board and offered it at a discount. It didn't belong on the Oops board. The food was good. But the cafe was cold, and the discount was my way of making things up to my customers. I would have offered complimentary coffee, but after switching to an expensive brand, I simply couldn't afford to.

Susie walked in the door of the café just as I was putting my latest mocha chocolate bundt cake under a glass dome on the counter across from the grill. Without asking what she needed, I whipped the glass dome back off, cut her a big piece, and then offered the option of cold milk or hot coffee. On the house. Murder suspects whom I believed to be innocent would always eat on the house at my cafe.

"Coffee," Susie said, sounding as forlorn and haggard as she looked.

I poured her a large cup and then set the cream and sugar out next to it. When she didn't move to finish the coffee off herself, I did it for her, doing my best to duplicate the coffee-cream-brown sugar ratio that I'd seen her use.

"I told all my customers about your coffee," Susie said.

"Have you opened your shop back up yet?" I asked, feeling hopeful. She looked so depressed. But if her shop was open, it was a good sign that she was managing herself okay.

"No..."

My hopes were dashed against the rocks and drowned in an icy sea. I pulled my cardigan tighter around me. I had the fireplace in the cozy corner going full tilt. Between the activity and the baking, I'd been comfortable enough prior to Susie coming in, but she brought a hopelessness with her that sucked all the warmth away.

No other customers were in yet, and Brenda hadn't left. I told Brenda to take care of any customers who came in—which she grumbled about—and I marched Susie back to the cozy corner and sat her down into the snuggliest chair. Next came a white afghan decorated with giant yellow daisies. I put the chocolate cake and coffee next to her and ordered, "Eat."

She did eat, lifelessly at first. Then she drank her coffee. Then she ate some more cake. The color slowly returned to her cheeks. She no longer blinked in slow motion. And without even seeming to move, she sat up taller. She was back.

"The police think I did it," Susie finally said.

Been there. Done that. Zoey and I had both stared down that particular barrel of a gun—sometimes literally.

"What makes them think it was a murder and not an accident?" I know that Derek had called it murder, but if he didn't do it and didn't see it, there was a chance it could have been an accident instead.

"I don't know. Nobody would tell me anything."

"Did you do it?" It was a question that had to be asked.

Susie's eyes welled with tears and she shook her head no. "I let them take my fingerprints yesterday. They're going to find my fingerprints all over that shredder that killed Mr. Pratt. But I didn't do it. I went into his office, saw him, ran over and tried to pull the shredder off of him. It was right up against his face. It was terrible! I tried to get it off, but it wouldn't budge. That's when I realized they were locked together. I ran after out after that. Ran as fast as I could. Mr. Pratt was dead. Really dead. Like… I don't know, *dead*. No CPR will do kind of dead. I've never seen anything like that before. He wet himself, did you know that?"

I shook my head.

"It wasn't like what you see on the TV." Susie seemed to shrink into herself again, growing pale, and I nudged her cup of coffee a little closer to her. She drank and seemed to recover. She took a deep breath. Without looking at me, she revealed the thing that seemed to be sitting on her the heaviest. "I had a fight with Mr. Pratt earlier in the day. When I found him, that was the second time I'd been there." She looked at me. "I was so mad, Kylie. I was yelling. I called him names. I told him that I wouldn't let him get away with it. He was trying to ruin me on purpose, Kylie. I figured it out."

"What do you mean?"

"He'd found out my business was doing better, that business was picking up, and that's why he raised the rent. He said he didn't like his tenants to get too far above themselves, liked to remind them who they were, keep 'em down and struggling."

My mouth fell open. "He said that?"

Susie hedged, rocking her head from side to side. "Not in those words, but that was the message. Kylie, I'd never been so mad in my life. I was seeing red. When I left, if I'd had a gun, I might have used it. If I'd have had anything—a crowbar—I would have busted his office to pieces."

"Why'd you go back?"

Susie repositioned herself in the overstuffed chair. She looked more energized, empowered even. "I went back to his office to tell him that he wasn't going to get one more red cent out of me. Not one.

He could go ahead and sue. He could do whatever he wanted. And, if he won the lawsuit, I'd file for bankruptcy so that he still wouldn't get anything. I'd make sure that everything I had went to cover lawyer's fees and that there'd be nothing left to pay him."

"Wow…" What she was talking about was hardcore. She'd been ready to turn her entire world upside down and rip it apart rather than give Mr. Pratt any more money. Sadly, that wasn't doing anything to convince me that she wasn't the murderer. If anything, I was seeing some of that passion that Brad had been talking about. But was it a killing passion?

Susie nodded. "Yeah. Wow. My sweet-heart, Sam, asked me to move in with him. Well, first he got down on one knee and asked me to marry him, but I told him that I didn't want to bring my legal problems onto him. So then he asked me to move in with him. He said he'd build me my own private salon space in the house, with its own garden-level entrance and everything. He's a carpenter, so he can do that kind of thing. He described it all, said he'd do anything for me, and that he loved me."

Tears were in Susie's eyes, but I was still stuck on her saying that Sam would do anything for her. I'd seen his picture when Susie had cut and colored my hair. He was a big guy. A strong guy. Strong enough to hold Mike Pratt down while the shredder choked the life out of him by eating his scarf.

I had a new suspect.

"He said he didn't want to be without me, said he'd been planning to ask me to marry him in another month after he got the ring but that he saw no reason to wait. He'd been planning on building me that salon all along. Said he was grateful to Mr. Pratt 'cause it gave me a little more incentive to say yes." Susie laughed with tearful joy. "The silly fool. I'd have said yes anyway."

Maybe I didn't have a new suspect. Then again, sounded like Sam had been ready to shake Mike's dead hand. But, if the threat of a lawsuit was getting in the way of their impending nuptials, maybe Sam would see to Mike's end after all.

The mental tennis match of lobbing Sam back and forth as a suspect in my head was giving me a headache. I decided to put a pin in the idea and circle back to it if we ran into a dead end.

Susie reached out a hand and touched mine, pulling me back into the moment. "I don't want you investigating this, hun," she said.

"Huh?" I hadn't seen that coming.

"I don't want you investigating this," she said again. "Somebody killed Mr. Pratt, and that somebody is dangerous. If they killed Mr. Pratt, they might try to kill you, and I've only just found you as a friend. I don't want to lose you."

I decided to play dumb. "What makes you think I'd investigate?" Susie made a face at me, one that chided, "Come on." She wasn't buying my innocent act. Still, I wasn't sure if I was being warned off because she was guilty or because she was legitimately concerned about my safety. Or... was it both?

"You investigated Rachel's murder to clear your name," Susie said. "Then you investigated Cam's to clear Zoey's name. Now, just like a cold that's getting past around, it's my turn, but I don't want you looking into it. I want you to stay clear."

"But I don't understand why."

"Just please," Susie said, "leave this one alone."

CHAPTER 5

With Susie having gone on her way, I was left to ponder all that she'd said to me. Zoey and I had managed to clear our names of murder when we were innocent. Yet Susie wanted me to stay away. That had me wondering: was Susie innocent?

I was mindlessly wiping down the counters, lost in thought, when Brad walked in. He took a seat across from me, and I enjoyed watching his incredibly athletic body move beneath the thin fabric of his uniform. Albeit there wasn't much to see. He had his jacket on. It stopped me from being able to appreciate all of what good genes and good habits had done for him.

"What's on the menu today?" he asked.

"You missed breakfast. You're late." I was stating the obvious, and he hadn't missed breakfast. I'd make him his usual eggs now if he wanted.

"I had to be at the court this morning. Had to testify at a hearing."

"Anybody I know?" I asked.

"More like somebody who wishes you didn't know them," Brad said with a smile. Then he shrugged. "It didn't go well for them."

I was glad. Zoey and I had made an enemy when solving Cameron Caldwell's murder. I'd be able to sleep better knowing there were walls, bars, and armed guards between us.

From his seat, Brad talked me through making a pot of coffee just as he would do it. When done, I poured him a cup. Then I got him a plate of the meal of the day. It was loaded potato soup with grated cheese and crumbled bacon on top. It was served with crostini that had been topped with garlic-infused oil. Brenda had guided me in making the soup, and then I'd practiced toasting the bread until I got it right. She'd made the garlic oil.

Brad leaned over the dish and breathed it in deep. Then he took a bite. "Mmm, I should come late more often."

Compliments from Brad came far and few between, and I embraced that one as a good one.

Agatha came in, and I got her a bowl of soup as well. She put on reading glasses and slid them to the end of her nose, pulled out a book and started reading. An actual book with actual pages. It had been ages since I'd seen anyone do that.

With Agatha occupying herself, I took the opportunity to gently pry Brad for information.

"Have you learned anything more about what happened to Mike Pratt?"

With his head down over his soup, Brad looked up at me past his eyebrows. "I shouldn't have talked to you about that," he said. "I was runnin' my mouth, and I knew better."

I gave a one-shouldered shrug, aiming for nonchalance. "You didn't say anything that everyone didn't already know." It was time to give a little to get a little. If I got him talking, maybe he'd say more than he meant to. "Susie was in here this morning."

Brad put down his spoon. "Oh, yeah? How'd that go?"

I shrugged again. "She was a bit deflated, but I perked her up with some chocolate cake."

"Hey, is that the same chocolate cake you made the other day? You got any left? Can I take a piece to go?"

My heart swelled and I had to fight to keep from getting all giddy and smiley. Brad liked my cake.

"Doris on dispatch had a birthday yesterday and I forgot to get her a card or anything. I figured that cake would be okay in a pinch."

All my happiness escaped. It was my turn to be deflated.

"You're a cruel man, Brad Calderos," I said.

Despite her apparent attention being on her book, Agatha chuckled.

Brad glanced at her. "Agatha's a good kid. Knows when to stay out of things." He said the last looking straight at me. He was baiting me. Goading me.

Game on.

I leaned onto my arms, perching them on the counter. "I'm going to investigate Mike Pratt's murder." I purred the words. Dangled them out in front of him.

Brad's eyes narrowed. "I knew it. You just can't keep out of stuff that has nothing to do with you. Got to be Little Miss Busybody."

"I'm going to figure out who the killer is before you do."

"Not a chance," he said, leaning forward.

"I did it before. Twice."

"No, you didn't. You just made such a God awful nuisance of yourself until the killer decided to kill you next. Until then, you didn't have a clue."

"If I didn't have a clue, how'd I manage to make a nuisance of myself with the killer?"

"Luck. The dumb kind," he said.

"I might be a brilliant idiot, but at least I'm still brilliant. What are you?"

Agatha slapped her book down on to the counter. "Are you going to pull her piggy tails next, Brad? And what about you, Kylie? Are you going to kick him in the knee and then kiss him?"

I gasped, but Brad chuckled. "She's got your number," he gloated, but the gloating was short lived because Agatha hit him on the head with her book.

"Hey! Assaulting an officer is a crime, you know."

"And what will you do about it?" Agatha asked, looking at him over the rim of her glasses.

Brad cleared his throat, then coughed into his hand before choking out, "Nothing."

Agatha went back to reading, and I decided to press Brad one more time. I was hoping Agatha's assault on his pride had eroded his defenses.

"Mike Pratt," I said. "Have you gotten the fingerprint results back on the comparison to Susie?"

"Not yet."

"They're Susie's," I said. "She told me all about it."

Brad's brows went up. "She confessed to you about killing Mike Pratt?"

I shook my head. "No, she confessed to trying to save his life."

Brad scoffed.

"She went into his office and found him on the floor with the shredder on top of him," I said.

"Yeah, yeah… I've heard the story. I'm not buying it. Too convenient."

"A person trying to save another person's life is too convenient?"

"When you're a cop, yeah. It is. The stuff I've seen, Kylie. The things people have done, and the excuses they come up with to explain away the evidence." He leaned forward. "You know the difference between reality and all those crime shows on TV?"

I shook my head.

"In real life, the most likely suspect almost always did it. If the wife got killed with a shotgun and the husband keeps one in the closet, well guess what… the husband did it. Not the dog. Not the kid next door. Not the nosy neighbor from down the street. The husband."

"Mike Pratt wasn't married." I didn't know if he was or not, but I hadn't heard anyone even once mention a wife, so I decided to take a shot in the dark.

"Don't matter. Whoever is the most likely suspect most likely did it. Right now, Susie's our girl. She's got motive, means and opportunity." He ticked them off on his fingers as he said them. "She was there at his office the day he died. He was hiking up her rent up to extortion-level prices. And he liked to wear that ridiculously long scarf wrapped around his neck. It's like he was begging for somebody to kill him, and our girl Susie just complied. Now that's the way it happened, isn't it? She confessed to you, didn't she?" He was nodding his head as if him nodding would get me to nod and confirm his theory.

"Not. Even. Close." I sucked in a breath to tell Brad about Susie's brand new fiancé, but stopped. What if her fiancé killed Mike in a misguided attempt to protect Susie and his future with her? As wrong as it was—if that was what he'd done—I wasn't ready to put a finger of guilt at him. I liked Susie, too, and I felt more than a little bit protective of her. Could I fault the man who loved her and wanted to spend the rest of his life with her for having similar yet more intense feelings?

I knew the answer to that question even if I didn't like it. Whoever killed Mike, no matter who it was, they had to be held accountable. Even if it was Susie herself. After all, she'd even joked about planning to kill Mike a couple of days before his death.

In the end, I stopped trying to pry Brad for information. I was getting nothing from him, and I was on the verge of giving information away. While I wanted the killer to be caught, I didn't want to point a finger at someone before I was sure.

I got Brad his piece of cake and sent him on his way.

"You're trying to help Susie, aren't you?" Agatha asked. She'd put down her book and she had a twinkle in her eye. "You knew more than you were saying to Brad."

I blew out a tired breath. "I do, Agatha!"

"And you're going to investigate."

"I am..." I said it in the same way a person might admit to having a crush on someone they didn't want to have a crush on. And I was starting to have such doubts about Brad. We'd found ourselves in adversarial positions to each other over and over again since having met. We could never get on the same side of an argument.

Agatha sighed, her eyes looking dreamy. "The sparks that are gonna fly between you and Brad if you solve another murder before him."

"He'll never forgive me, will he?"

Agatha laughed. "Mmmm, don't you worry about that. Some men run away from a strong woman, but that man is like a moth drawn to a flame." She took my hand and squeezed it. "You keep shining just as bright as you want to, honey. He's not going anywhere."

I wasn't sure what to think about that, didn't have time to process it... before Bruce and Maryanne—my ex's parents—walked through the café door, holding up a phone in the middle of a video call. Dan's smiling mug took up the whole thing.

"Kylie! Baby! There's my girl!" he said.

"I'm dating Brad!" I blurted. Joel was walking into the café behind Dan's parents, and I pointed my finger so emphatically that it was more like jabbing it through the air. I cried out, "And Joel, too! I'm dating both of them! I have two boyfriends!"

CHAPTER 6

It was not one of my finer moments. I had grabbed Joel with both hands and tossed him right under the bus—the I'm-not-yours-anymore, will-never-be-yours-again bus that I was trying to make painfully clear to Dan and his parents. Joel's expression went from blank to smiling in under half a second.

"Sweetheart," he said, moving around Bruce and Maryann to stand next to me where I'd come out from behind the grill's bar. He snuggled up against me and slid his arm low around my waist. He turned to the phone, still held up by Maryann. "There's the man I want to thank!" Joel boomed, pulling me closer against him. "Your loss—my gain. You know how it goes."

Dan was no longer smiling. After nine years of marriage, I knew his expressions well. His face was stoic, but his eyes were blazing. "Well, wasn't that fast," he said drolly. "Didn't take you long to pillow hop."

My eyes bulged and my mouth fell open. "Excuse me?" So many things went through my head, and then my sense of self-preservation kicked in. I looked around me. Besides Dan, Dan's parents, Joel, and Agatha, there were a few other customers scattered throughout the café. All eyes were on me. If I made a scene, if I aired my dirty laundry for all to hear, that's exactly what would happen. All would hear about it. And with phone cameras the way they were, with my luck I'd end up on YouTube telling Dan off for being a womanizing, self-centered, egotistical, no good ex-husband who had slept with half of the eastern seaboard. A million views later and I could kiss my dream of a happy, healthy, cozy and sweet café goodbye. Instead of being known for having good food (hey, a girl can dream), it would be known for being owned by the woman who thought she was on stage at a Jerry Springer show.

So, instead of unloading months of intense anger, pain and humiliation, I instead smiled bright, patted Joel on the side, and asked, "Have you met my boyfriend, Joel? I told him about Mom's pot roast, and he's looking forward to a great big sit down meal together."

Maryann squeaked. Her eyes were bulging, and I wasn't sure she was still breathing. She was a nice woman. She'd always been good to me. And I felt bad about subverting the dinner she had planned. I'm sure she had imagined how the evening would go. Dan would be charming. I'd swoon. We'd go off for a chat to work things out, and then we'd come back ten minutes later to announce that I was pregnant with twin grandbabies, a girl and a boy. Joel was a definite kink in the future she had envisioned. Of course, Dan cheating with enough women to fill a banquet hall hadn't fit in with my life plans either.

Dan narrowed his eyes and leaned into the camera. "How old is he? He's too young for you."

"He's *my* age!" I said, offended. I didn't actually know how old Joel was. I glanced up at him, and he nodded agreement.

Dan was nine years older than me. My guess was that he didn't like seeing me with another man younger than him and that his complaint had next to nothing to do with how old I was versus how old Joel was. It was about how much younger Joel was than Dan.

"You're embarrassing yourself, Kylie. People are going to talk. And what will Mom and Dad think?"

"Dan, they're *your* Mom and Dad!" I regretted the words instantly, but it was too late. Maryann's eyes started filling with tears. "Mom... Mom... I'm sorry. I didn't mean it. You'll always be dear to me, no matter how much of a dumb—"

"Sweetheart," Joel interrupted with a

squeeze. "Maybe you would like to host your ex and your, uh, parents here at the café. You could cook dinner for all of us."

Dan fell silent. Maryann's unshed tears got stunned into submission. Bruce coughed and then said, "Now, now. No reason to go to extremes." He froze as he seemed to realize the insult of his words.

"It'd be great!" Joel beamed. "With you hosting it here, Brad could come too. That way you'd have all your fellas around you."

More coughing from the Hibberts.

I latched on to the life raft that Joel was throwing me. "I could make chicken cacciatore!"

"Honey, Kylie," Maryann said, "let's think a moment. Salmonella is such a risk these days. Dan was in the hospital for so long after the Thanksgiving turkey."

"That wasn't my fault," I blurted, my cheeks turning hot. I turned to Joel. "Honest, that wasn't my fault."

"It's okay, babe. You make turkey. You make chicken. You make blowfish. I'm there, and I'm having dinner with you."

He leaned down and gave me a kiss on my cheek, and I melted. If Dan, his mother and father, Agatha and the few other customers hadn't been around, I would have totally turned that cheek kiss into the kind of kiss that makes a school girl blush.

When I looked back toward Maryann and the phone she was holding up, Dan had hung up. He was gone.

I breathed a sigh of relief and leaned into Joel. My hero.

Looking disheartened, Maryann and Bruce left.

"You were a lifesaver, Joel. Thank you," I said.

Joel shoved his hands deep into his pockets and got an awww shucks look on his face. "Who would I be if I couldn't help a pretty girl out?" he said.

It was my turn to feel bashful and unsure of what to do with myself. Joel was a big guy. He had broad, thick shoulders and a tight waist. His build was somewhere between football player and runner. He was bigger than life. Yet here he was, with eyes for me. That's when I realized, even the bigger-than-life guys need someone to cuddle up with on a long, cold night.

Just like that Joel shifted from out-of-reach superhero to snuggly teddy bear. Approachable. Loveable. And, yes, even attainable.

"You know," he said, "I still haven't taken you out on that date."

"Yeah," I laughed. "All those pesky murderers getting in the way."

Joel's expression changed. He went from looking like an overgrown kid to a man on a mission. "Speaking of murderers, what do you know about Michael Pratt's murder?"

Ahhhh, I thought to myself. I was no longer talking to Joel the suitor. I was talking to Joel the newspaper man.

"You grab a seat at the bar's grill, I'll get you some lunch, and I'll fill you in on what I know." That wasn't the complete truth. I'd fill Joel in on what I thought that I could tell him, which was less than what I knew—or rather what I suspected.

Joel sat and I got him a big bowl of potato soup with grated cheese sprinkled on top. I added to that a great big piece of my mocha chocolate cake. I loved that I'd finally figured out how to bake a cake and bake it well, but I was concerned that I was going to wear my customers out with only having the one and same dessert option available day after day. I guessed that I could mix it up by adding some nuts on one day and some chopped chocolate on another, but at the end of the day, it would still be the same mocha chocolate cake they'd been eating.

"I've been thinking about this cake all morning," Joel said as he cut himself a big forkful before even trying his soup. When he put it in his mouth and closed his eyes, he looked as though he were in heaven.

"Joel," I laughed, "you always know the perfect thing to say!"

"What kind of a newspaper guy would I be if I didn't?" he said, giving me a wink. "Now you tell me what you know about Mike Pratt's death."

"Is this for a big scoop? You going to do a big write-up?"

"I'm working on a story."

"Will you be sure not to mention my name specifically?"

Joel's brows went up. "You don't want the free publicity?" His voice took on the hollow sound of a professional commentator or news anchor. *"According to Kylie Berry, owner and operator of Sarah's Eatery, Mike Pratt was the victim of a love triangle gone wrong."*

My eyes went wide. "Was he?" I hadn't even considered the possibility that he'd been killed because of a romantic relationship. It had never even occurred to me to consider that it could be something other than his heavy-handed and unscrupulous business practices.

"No, no… at least not that I know of," Joel said.

My shoulders sagged. "You got me all excited there." If he had been killed because of a love triangle, I was pretty sure that Susie wouldn't have been a part of it. She seemed over the moon for her guy.

Joel took a bite of his soup. Surprise registered on his face. "This is good!"

"Thanks!" More warm inner glow and happiness. Joel was as good as Santa at Christmas.

"This tastes a lot like a soup my mom makes, except that she puts in a lot of sweet onion so that it's almost more of an onion potato soup than straight potato."

"Is it good?"

"Real good."

"I'll try that next time I make it."

"Let me know and I'll help. I'll get the recipe from her."

Tingles and anticipation filled me. Alone in a kitchen standing close to Joel. Tasting the soup together. Him standing behind me, putting his arms around me to show me the best way to cut an onion.

"Now, about Mike Pratt," Joel said, all business again. "What do you know?"

Strategy time. I wasn't sure what I should say and what I shouldn't say. Joel and his very public stories could ruin someone's life just as much as Brad and his badge could.

"You first," I said.

"Ohhh, that how we going to play this?" Joel asked with a smile that reached his eyes. "You're investigating again, aren't you." It was more of a statement than a question, but then he asked, "Why?"

"Susie Prescott is a friend of mine. I'm guessing you've heard that she's a suspect?"

Joel nodded. "From what I've heard, she's *the* suspect."

"Yeah, well, isn't that the problem? If the police aren't looking at anyone else, then they won't find anyone else, but I don't think she did it."

"Don't think she did it? Or don't want her to have done it?"

I pulled my mouth sideways, hating to admit that he was right. "I don't want her to have done it," I finally admitted.

"Is there someone you do want to have done it?"

"That's such a terrible question."

"I know... But is there?"

"No, just more of the same. People that I hoped didn't do it."

"And who might some of those people be?"

Ohhhh, Joel was good. Very, very good. "I see what you did," I teased.

Joel shrugged with a smile and ate some more of his soup.

"What are the suspects that you have in mind for killing Mike?"

"I've been asking around. Turns out Mike wasn't that popular of a guy. What he did to Susie—jacking up her rent as soon as her business started doing better and locking her into an unfair contract—he'd tried to that before to other people. A bunch of times."

"Did he always succeed?"

"Nope, not always. Some would refuse to sign the contract unless changes were made, so they'd head off the problem at the pass. Others, they'd pay and then move their shop to somewhere else as soon as they could, and at least a few people ruined their own business base so that they were barely making a profit and then convinced him that they weren't doing so well in the business after all. As long as a person was barely making it, he tended to leave their rent alone."

"How did he ever get anyone to rent from him?" I felt bewildered at the blatant abuses the man had wielded.

Joel shrugged. "Mike could be mean. Most people didn't want to make an enemy of him, so they'd act like everything was fine and that they'd had a good business relationship with him."

"It sounds like the police should have a long list of possible murderers."

Joel did a sideways nod. "I don't know. Most people had already figured out how to manage Mike and their troubles with him were part of the past. They had no reason to go after him."

I crossed my arms and leaned my hip into the counter. "But Susie's problems weren't sorted yet, were they? She was still in a difficult situation and Mike was the one making it difficult." Silently, though, I wondered if that were true. She *had* sorted it out. She'd decided to embrace financial ruin rather than pay him any more. She'd made a choice, had possibly even been at peace with it. But I wondered, had her fiancé been as at peace with it as she had?

CHAPTER 7

With Joel out the door, that left just me and Agatha. She was halfway through her book and on her third cup of coffee. With her reading glasses balanced on the end of her nose and her gold, dangling earrings each swinging a little green gem, she looked somewhere between schoolmarm and chic chick. Amazingly, her pixie cut white hair complimented either look perfectly.

"Not that I don't love your company, but what has you hanging out here so long today?"

Agatha put down her book. "My knitting group will be here soon. I'm enjoying this book so much that I wanted to get some reading in before they came. Not to mention, I'm loving this cake you made." She pinched off a small bite and popped it in her mouth.

I leaned to the side and craned my neck, doing my best to see around the back corner spot in the café. The spot I called the Cozy Corner. I smiled. It was empty, which meant that I wasn't going to need to come up with some elaborate ruse to vacate the space so that the ladies could relax near the fireplace in the over-stuffed chairs.

I loved that Agatha brought her knitting group and also her book club here. More than once I'd seen some of the members of each group come in at times without the others, and rarely were they alone. They almost always brought a friend or a family member. It was word of mouth advertising for the café, and that was the best kind. It was free, passive, and the most trusted by new customers.

"I do feel for you, dear," Agatha said.

"Huh?" I'd been so absorbed with my

thoughts of flying dollar bills from all the passive advertising that I was encouraging that I'd stopped paying attention to my actual in-the-flesh customer… and friend.

"Having to deal with your ex that way… and all his family. You moved all the way across the country to little Camden Falls but he's still not done with you."

"Oh, Agatha," I laughed. "Dan is sooo done with me. Beyond done with me. I mean, the man all but spit at me as I walked out his door. He burned every bridge I had. He left me with nothing."

Agatha looked at me over the rim of her glasses. "Little boys pulling pigtails," she said in a sing-song voice.

My jaw dropped. "No, no way. That wasn't pulling pigtails. That was running over me with a Mack truck and then backing up over me just to make sure he'd done the job right. The way he treated me, that wasn't because he loved me."

"You're right," Agatha declared. "It was

because he didn't like losing something he considered *his*."

Well, she had me there. Dan never had liked losing. Not at golf. Not at charades. Not at cards. And certainly not at anything having to do with me.

"Yeah," I said with a hand wave, "but that's all meaningless now. He's in the past. I'm in the past. Our paths are completely divergent. There's nothing but space between us. Nothing shared except me seeing his parents from time to time."

"His business is going under."

They were such simple words, but it was like a bomb went off in my head. Fear shot through my spine, and the words, "Oh my gosh, what will we do!" filled my head. I'd even forgotten to breathe and didn't notice until my lungs started burning.

Then I did breathe, and I remembered. The business my ex-husband and I built together was not my business. It was his. *My* future didn't depend on it. His did. The relief and the ridiculousness of it all made me giddy, and I started to laugh. I could feel my face going hot and knew that it must be bright red, and my eyes filled with tears.

"Oh... oh," I said, swiping under my eye. "That feels so good. So amazing."

"It feels amazing that your ex-husband's business is going under?"

"Oh, no! No, not that." I couldn't stop smiling. "It feels amazing that it has absolutely nothing to do with me. I'm free."

Agatha pursed her lips. "Mmmhmm, word is that his father is considering retiring and that Dan might move back from Chicago to take over the family business."

My knees buckled and I hit the floor, but I was back on my feet no more than a second later. I did my best to pretend that nothing had happened.

Agatha's smile was quirked sideways. It was obvious that she was trying to give all her attention to her book, but I could tell that she was struggling not to look at me with a huge I-told-you-so grin.

Agatha's fellow knitters arrived and

she found her way to the cozy corner with them. I had to admit. I was feeling sullen. How dare Agatha point out how Dan was probably going to try to turn my life upside down and inside out all over again. I wanted to stand in the corner with my arms crossed and glare at her, but it was time for me to put on my big girl panties. The bearer of bad news didn't deserve my hostility. She deserved my thanks and my gratitude. Being forewarned was being forearmed, and I was going to knock Dan's head off if he tried to waltz himself back into my life. I'd moved on. I'd picked myself up, dusted myself off, and had made something of myself.

Okay, so maybe I hadn't *made* something of myself. Maybe I'd fallen into the best deal anyone could imagine with my good ol' friend nepotism, but still. I've had to show up for this opportunity. I've had to stretch outside my comfort zone and try to succeed in an area where I have failed my whole life. I now cooked for others and they *paid* me for the food that

I prepared for them. *Paid* me for it! The thought was enough to make me giggle. Once upon a time it would have made more sense for me to pay others to eat my food, not the other way around.

No, I'd come a long way and I'd done it without Dan. Whatever he was going through, whatever was falling apart in his life, he'd have to pick up the pieces without me.

The café's door chime rang, and I turned just in time to greet Zoey with a big smile. But behind her were three of my building's business owners—and they were not smiling. At all.

"Deirdre, Alex, Jacob," I said in greeting. "Can I get you some coffee? Maybe a piece of cake?" Their dour expressions didn't alter.

Deirdre was a dark-skinned goddess somewhere between thirty and sixty years old, Alex was a thirty-something blond-headed man with hair that seemed to keep trying to turn red, and Jacob was something between a bookworm and a psychopath. He just had that indeterminate look about him that made me think he could go either way.

Deirdre stepped to the front of the trio, and Alex and Jacob flanked her, crossing their arms over their chests. While I'm sure the threat was symbolic and not literal, it was clear that the two men were there as Deirdre's muscle. That the three of them were there in solidarity didn't seem to be good enough. They wanted to physically intimidate as well.

"What's up?" I asked, address Deirdre since she was clearly their spokesperson.

"What's up is that we are losing customers," Deirdre answered curtly. "Our businesses are cold. Poor Jacob has had half of his customers walk in, stay for two minutes, complain about the temperature and then leave."

I glanced at Jacob in anticipation of him saying something to back up this claim, but he merely pursed his lips, squinted his eyes, and gave one silent nod of his head. Jacob owned a medical supply store. They sold everything from compression hoses to the types of beds that were found inside of a hospital, but his equipment was destined for home use.

When it was clear that Jacob wasn't going to add anything to Deirdre's claim, I said, "I'm very sorry to hear about that, Jacob. I—"

"Alex has lost nearly as many customers," Deirdre said, cutting me off.

That Alex was also losing customers really surprised me. He was the owner-operator of an architectural firm. I couldn't imagine a person going with a different designer on a building structure just because they needed to layer with an extra sweater for a few hours. "I'm really sorry to hear about that, Al—"

"And I have lost over seventy-five percent of my customers," Deirdre said, cutting me off again. She had one of those stage voices that carried, and my ears flinched each time she hit a hard consonant.

"I'm really sorry, Deirdre. I—"

"SORRY isn't good enough," Deirdre said.

If she cut me off one more ti—

"Your apologies mean nothing to us. *We* want to know what you're going to do about it."

I looked to the still silent Alex and Jacob. For people so determined to know what I was going to do about it, they hadn't said one word. Maybe Deirdre wouldn't let them. I got the sudden image of her as their queen bee with Alex and Jacob her dutiful drones.

"I—"

"We *refuse* to be treated this way."

"I—"

"We have rights as your tenants and our next action will be to seek legal counsel."

"I—"

"If you do not addr—"

"Would you like some hot cocoa?" I blurted, interrupting Deirdre.

"W—"

"I'm about to make it fresh."

"Tha—"

"Please," I motioned to the counter. "Take a seat."

"Th—"

"Now." Deirdre and her cronies had worn out my last nerve. Thankfully, I didn't need to push the point any harder. They looked at each other. I saw a few of their imaginary chips fall off their shoulders. Then, they took seats at the grill's counter.

I didn't have any hot cocoa made yet, so I went with coffee instead and gave Deirdre, Alex and Jacob each a big slice of chocolate cake. I waited for them all to take a bite. I watched the magic of chocolate soothe their features. Then, I said, "I'm sorry about the heat in your businesses. And I'm sorry that I haven't been able to afford to supply you with space heaters to stave off the cold. I have a local company working on the replacement of the building's boiler right now, and according to their latest progress report, they are on schedule. Heat should be returning to the building in another week."

"That's all well and good," Alex said, speaking for the first time, "but we want to know what you're going to do to offset our losses."

They were going to hit me up for money. Money I didn't have. I broke out in the flush of a cold sweat. This was a shakedown.

Deirdre put her fork down onto the cake's plate with a clank. "We want a fifteen percent discount on our rent for the next three months to make up for the losses incurred by your failure to maintain the minimum level of comfort within the building."

Soooo many things went through my head. None of them were nice. Then the image of Mike's prone and strangled body being wheeled out of his office filled my mind. I wasn't afraid of Deirdre, Alex or Jacob killing me. I wasn't even afraid of them trying to kneecap me in some abandoned dark alley. I wasn't even afraid that they'd drag their keys down the side of my car—if I had a car. But what I was afraid of was becoming like Mike.

Petty. Tight. Abusive.

I did not want to be the landlord that

Mike had been. I did not want to be the type of person he had been. I wanted to be someone much, much different.

"Twenty percent off," I said, and watched their slow, satisfied smiles grow, "for one month and one month only."

"That is unacceptable!" Deidre snapped.

"Twenty-five percent, and that's my final offer," I said. "If this conversation continues, I will withdraw the offer."

Without saying a word, Deirdre looked at Alex. They nodded. Then she looked at Jacob. Another duo-nod.

Then, with a big toothy smile, Deirdre extended a hand to me to shake. I took it. "It's a deal," she said.

The trio got up from their stools and headed for the door. That's when I heard a voice that was not Deirdre's and was not Alex's. It was Jacob. "And you guys thought we wouldn't get anything," he said, only to be hush hissed by Deirdre. Reaching the door, as if to cover for Jacob's comment, she turned, smiled and waved when she reached the door. She looked like a beauty pageant winner waving a float.

Then they were gone. I stared after them. Zoey sidled up next to me to look at the now vacant door with me.

"You got played," she said.

"I want to investigate Mike's murder."

"I thought you might."

"Think Susie did it?" I asked.

"Could my answer stop you from investigating?"

"No," I answered.

"Then, yes. I think she did it."

CHAPTER 8

Telling Susie that we were going to investigate Mike Pratt's murder was out of the question. She'd already told me her feelings on the matter: she wanted me to stay out of it. Yet doing the opposite somehow felt right. But one way or another, no matter what outcome, Zoey and I were going to find out what happened.

"Come on," I said. "Help me figure out how to make some hot cocoa."

Zoey and I headed into the kitchen. Zoey used her phone to look up hot cocoa recipes, and we chose one together. Zoey then navigated me through making the recipe. She had to stop me from substituting salt for sugar. Twice. With it done, I went rogue and added tiny marshmallows. I loved tiny marshmallows in hot cocoa. Nothing said home more to me than that.

With a serving tray decked from edge to edge with cup-topped saucers full of hot cocoa, we headed out to spend time with the ladies of Agatha's knitting group. She had with her the tall sixty-something sisters, Nancy and Shelly. Their long fingers worked nimbly on their respective projects. Nancy was working on a red and white gingham blanket and Shelly was working on an infant's pink sweater.

In addition to Nancy and Shelly was a new woman who I'd never met before. In contrast to Nancy and Shelly's long-legged height, this new woman was diminutive and delicate. She looked as though she belonged as the tiny figurine spinning in a music box.

"This is Prudence," Agatha said by way of introduction to the newest member.

"And of course you already know Nancy and Shelly."

I waved to the sisters, and then to Prudence, I said, "Hi."

She gave a smile and a nod in reply. Her fingers never stopped working, and her knitting needles never stopped their rhythmic clicking. I guessed her to be in her mid-thirties.

The collective click-click of their needles as they knit was soothing, and I realized that if given the chance, I could sit and listen to them as I drifted off to sleep. But I was here with ulterior motives: Zoey and I wanted information.

Together, Zoey and I put a cup of hot cocoa on whatever side table was nearest each woman. The whole time, Agatha watched us, looking like the cat that ate the canary. Her mouth was full of unspoken words.

When done passing out the hot cocoa, Zoey and I snuggled onto a loveseat together. I imagined sitting there on a cold, snowy night in front of the crackling fireplace with one of my suiters. I tried to picture which one it might be, and my mental image flickered between the handsome, athletic Brad and the steady, gentle giant Joel. But Dan's grinning face infiltrated and took over the image like a virus, rewriting what I saw in my head until the only thing that was left was him.

What I wouldn't give for a mental scouring pad. I wondered if I'd be able to drink the image of Dan away, or if maybe I could have him erased with the help of a hypnotherapist. At this point I was ready to try anything. Whatever it took to keep Dan out of my head and most definitely out of my life.

"What would you ladies like to know?" Agatha asked, pulling me out of my thoughts and back into the moment.

"Can't we just want to spend time in your company?" I asked. I hated being so transparent.

Agatha laughed. "Admit it. You want to know about Mike Pratt."

"Ohhhh, Mike... That's some juicy gossip," Prudence said, her eyes going large and round. "I heard that he was killed by the brother of a woman he'd jilted from Russia." She nodded her head with slow, exaggerated confidence, her eyes as large as ever. "Mail order bride."

"Prude," Nancy chided, "that was from a Lifetime movie that aired two nights ago."

Prudence's head jerked back and her gaze darted this way and that as if searching for something inside her head. Finally, the light dawned. "Ohhhhh," she said. "You're right." She smiled large and went back to knitting.

I was speechless. I didn't know what to say. How does one follow that up?

"I had Mike in a kindergarten class that I substituted for," Sally said. "Their regular teacher was on maternity leave. It was a hard pregnancy at the end, and I had the class for four months."

"What was Mike like as a little boy?" I asked.

"Very sweet. Maybe a little too sensitive. But he was very generous. He'd cut out flowers from the construction paper and give them away, share his toys, console other children when they were crying. He was never a problem. If other children squabbled, he'd try to make things better."

I knew that that had been a long time ago, but it didn't sound anything like the man who Susie had described. The Mike that she had described was opportunistic and mean. He was a person eager to take advantage of others. "Are you sure we're talking about the same person?" I asked.

"Oh yes, yes," Sally said. Her shining, metallic, fluorescent pink knitting needles never missed a beat. They kept clicking, and Sally's yarn kept moving through them. It amazed me that a single piece of string could be tied in so many little loose knots to create things so beautiful, intricate and unique. "It was him. Since his death I've heard a lot of things said about Mike, and I can hardly believe my ears. I don't know if he hit his head and changed or if some experience changed him along the way, but he grew up to be everything that he wasn't as a child."

"He won the lottery when he was twenty-one," Prudence said.

"Prude, are you sure that isn't from another movie?" Nancy asked.

"No, no," Prudence said, shaking her head. "It was Mike, and it happened. He was about twenty-one and he was one of two people with the winning number of a Powerball jackpot. "He won millions."

My gut twisted. Mike had had wealth and ease fall into his lap, yet he'd gone out of his way to try to keep Susie and others, from what Joel told me, down. It was vile and petty, and it sounded nothing like the child that Sally had described.

"I don't think he lived lavishly," Sally said.

"No, he has a nice house, but it's not a mansion, and he drives an old truck. Been driving the same truck for years. For as long as I can remember, actually."

"I bet that's the same truck that he bought when he won the lottery," Agatha said. "And remember him getting one and driving it around. He was so proud. Told everyone how lucky he was."

Uh oh. "So he talked a lot about his winnings?"

"Mmhmm," Agatha said. "He'd tell anybody he met on the street. He was so happy. So proud. I was out to dinner one night at a restaurant with a gentleman caller, and Mike came in for dinner. He paid the bill for everybody there. He didn't do it for applause, either. He was quiet about it. We didn't find out until we got the check and it had 'gratis' written on it."

That sounded a lot like that little boy Sally had described having in kindergarten class. So, he managed to stay generous and nice until he'd won the lottery. It wasn't until after he'd won the lottery that his personality appears to have changed. And he wasn't secretive about his newfound wealth.

Very slowly, the puzzle pieces started to fit together in my mind. I arranged them this way and that, trying out the different variations. But no big picture sparks of insight came.

"He must have been smart about it," Prudence said.

"Huh?" She'd lost me with her unspoken jump in logic.

"A lot of windfall winners like that, they lose their money in a matter of years and end up as broke—or more broke—than they ever were. But Mike invested. He bought all those storefronts."

"How many did he own?" Zoey asked.

"I've no idea," Prudence said. "Nancy, do you know?" I wondered why Nancy might know, then Prudence answered that question for me. "Nancy's daughter dated Mike once upon a time."

"Oh..." My interest was piqued, but Nancy did a two-handed, knit-filled wave to dismiss the connection.

"That was years ago," Nancy said. "And Margot and Mike never got serious. They dated one summer, and then she left to go to a college out of state. It was all friendly and sweet. I'm not even sure they were exclusive with each other. I think that it might have been more like a group of friends hanging out together. He was sweet on her for a time, but then they both moved on with their lives at the end of summer."

"I can't say for sure," Agatha said, "but I think that he bought up a whole line of small storefronts on both sides of a street."

"Was it Brunt Street?" I asked. That was where Susie had her hair shop.

"Yes, that's the one."

"He spread out his investment risk," Zoey said.

"Huh?" I asked.

"He put his eggs in a lot of different baskets," Zoey said. "If one of the storefronts failed and the business owner closed up shop, he would only be hurt a little because he had several other renters at the same time. That was smart, especially for someone so young."

"But it also gave him more people he could wield influence over," I pointed out. "With multiple renters, there would be more opportunities to take advantage of someone."

"Kylie, that's dark," Sally said, but she nodded her head with approval.

"I know that his renters tended not to be happy with him," Agatha said.

"How do you know?" I asked.

"Mae Jensen owns the florist shop on that street, or rather she rented her space from Mike. A few years back, I was dating Mort, the funeral director at Benegan's Funeral Home."

"Wait a minute," I said, throwing up my hands, palms forward. "The funeral director's name was *Mort*?" It meant death in French.

"Yes," Agatha answered with a chuckle. "He thought it was funny. Anyway, Mae delivered most of the flowers to the funeral home. He told me that she complained about Mike every time she made a delivery."

"But that was a few years ago, right?" I asked.

"Mmhmm," Agatha said. Her knitting

needles slipped and slid past each other, never missing a stitch.

"And she still owns the same flower shop in the same spot?"

"I believe so," Agatha said.

"If she was having troubles with Mike all the way back then, why would she stay?"

Agatha shrugged. "Why would any of them stay? Susie has her shop on that road. Then there's Clara, we've already mentioned Mae, there's Betty, Robert, and Jasper. I don't know if they all rented from Mike, but they all have little shops on that road."

That was a lot of investigative legwork. At least Zoey and I would have people to talk to about Mike. Any one of those people could have been Mike's killer.

"I go to church with Mike's neighbor, Tina," Prudence said. "She *hated* him. Said he kept peeing on her hydrangeas."

"He what?" I couldn't believe my ears.

"She said he wouldn't even hide that he was doing it, either. She said he'd come out of his house in his robe to get his newspaper, then he'd walk over to the side of the yard that met up with hers, and he'd pee on her hydrangeas. She said he managed to kill two of the bushes that way." Prudence made a face. "Tina said she hired someone to replant new ones there rather than dig there herself."

Ewwww. Double ewwww.

But we had a new suspect: Tina, his neighbor. She had motive. Since Mike's office was in his converted garage, living next door to him gave her opportunity. And since Mike was killed by his own shredder strangling him with his own scarf, everybody had the means to kill him. Based on that alone, I could have killed him.

"Do you believe her claims about Mike?" Zoey asked.

"I don't know," Prudence said, making a face. "She's a bit of an odd duck. I usually try to avoid her, to be honest. You should have heard her describing Mike peeing on her flower bushes." Prudence gasped and then clucked her tongue.

"Such a vivid description. She even pantomimed it, right there as people were filing into church. I tell you what, I wanted to crawl off and hide under one of the pews."

I didn't know whether to laugh or be aghast.

"Did Mike have a girlfriend?" Zoey asked.

The four women looked at each other, as if doing a deep dive into their collective consciousness in search of the answer.

"Mmmm, not that I know of," Prudence finally answered.

"I only know of his ex," Nancy said. "I don't know how she knew, but Margot had heard he was with a woman named Emily and that they were engaged." Nancy shrugged. "But then there was no engagement announcement and no wedding, so I guess things didn't work out."

"How long ago was that?" I asked.

Nancy pursed her lips as she thought. "Nine, ten… maybe eleven or twelve years ago?" She framed it as a question even though it was answering a question that I'd asked.

"Does anyone know if Mike was still worth any money?" I asked.

"I'd figured he was," Prudence said.

"I never noticed any extravagances to prove it, but I always had the impression that he was doing well for himself," Nancy said.

"I heard he paid for a local girl's college tuition after her parents died in a car crash," Sally said. "That was a couple of years ago. Paid for all four years."

Generosity. From Mike. He was such a mixed bag.

"So, he still had money," Zoey said.

"Does anyone know who is due to inherit?"

All the ladies shook their heads. Nobody knew.

I asked the ladies if I could get them anything more from the kitchen, but they all declined. I put another small log on the fire, and then Zoey and I went back to the grill at the front of the café.

"Think you could find out what properties he owned?" I asked Zoey.

"What, you mean hack the County Clerk's Office records?"

I shrugged. "Or go down there and ask."

Zoey scrunched her face as if she found the idea distasteful. "I'll hack the records. Who do you think we should talk to first?"

"I think that the ex-girlfriend, Emily, is a great place to start. She liked him at one time at least. Would have had his confidences at some level. Maybe she can shed some light on what his life was like when he died."

"Emily it is."

CHAPTER 9

"Help me think of what I can make as a dinner dish," I said to Zoey.

"What's wrong with the potato soup you made? It was good and you made a lot. Don't you have some left?"

I started us walking toward the kitchen. "I do, but Agatha's already had the potato soup. She had it for lunch. I want her to be able to offer something different. Last time the knitters were here, they stayed almost four hours."

"What are you good at?" Zoey asked, climbing onto a tall stool inside the kitchen.

I gave her a sharp look. "Nothing. Have you met me?"

"That's not true. You made the potato soup. You've been making that chocolate cake. You even made hot cocoa."

"I would have ruined that hot cocoa if it hadn't been for you being here, setting me right whenever I was about to do something wrong."

"Well…" Zoey said.

She knew I had her. The debate was effectively won. I was a terrible cook. Yay me.

"Do you have any spaghetti?" she asked.

I made a face at her. "I'd like to avoid becoming known as the spaghetti queen."

"So I guess lasagna is out, too."

"Yep."

Zoey started surfing her phone, presumably looking up recipe options. "What kind of meat do you have?"

"I've got some chicken thighs and bacon."

Zoey did some more scrolling. "Do you have bourbon?" She paused and looked at me critically. "Tell me you have bourbon. We are in Kentucky. You gotta have bourbon."

"Um..." My mind raced. Then I snapped my fingers. "Yes! It's in the pantry." I felt so proud of myself, kind of like I'd actually just accomplished something, despite the fact that the bourbon was a carryover from when my cousin Sarah had owned the café.

"Then this is it." Zoey hopped down from the stool and showed me her phone's screen. "Bourbon-bacon barbecue sauce. You can make barbecue chicken."

I looked it over. "I think I can do this." Then, needing to feel more conviction with what I was saying, I said, "I can do this!" Of course, that didn't actually do anything to dispel my reservations—doubts based on years of botched cooking attempts. Zoey must have read it in my expression because she gave me a playful hip bump.

"I'll help," she said.

Zoey to the rescue, again.

We were in the kitchen cooking for two and a half hours. My waiter, Sam, had made it in to work and had been taking care of the customers while Zoey and I cooked. He peeped into the kitchen.

"People are starting to ask what you have cooking," he said. "It smells really good."

Zoey and I smiled at each other.

"If this turns out," I said, "it's a definite non-Oops board meal."

We left the oven to work its magic on the chicken, and Zoey and I headed back out to the grill, which opened up to the rest of the café. Zoey climbed up onto one of the grill's bar stools while I made a new pot of coffee.

"I can't believe you do this every day," she said. "My feet hurt."

I couldn't stop my smile and chuckled. "I'm sure that's got nothing to do with those five-inch platform heels of yours."

"Hey, these are comfortable," she said,

looking down at her feet. "Barely have any foot incline. All the height is in the sole."

I looked over as the café's front door chimed at a new arrival. It was a gentleman dressed in a three-quarter length coat over a light gray suit. He had an oval-shaped beard and mustache combo that I could best describe as dapper. His hair was salt and pepper, and stylishly combed back in a way that both flattered his features and softened his appearance. While not yet to the age of silver-fox, he looked very prepared to claim that title once he got there. Whoever the new customer was, he was very handsome in an old southern gentleman kind of way.

"Good morning, ladies," he said. He took off his coat and draped it over his arm before approaching the grill's bar to take a seat.

"Can I get you a cup of coffee?" I asked.

"I'd love that. Is there a menu? I've been on the road for a lot of hours today, and I could really do with a good meal."

I glanced nervously at Zoey. He'd said he wanted a "good" meal. He had to be from out of town. I was sure that everybody in town had by now heard that good was a pretty iffy proposition when eating at *Sarah's Eatery.*

I really needed to get around to changing the café's name...

I put on my best smile. "We don't have a menu other than a daily menu. Today we've got a loaded potato soup that's topped with crisp bacon and cheese. It's served with a toasted garlic crostini. And, in a little while, we'll have bourbon-bacon barbecue chicken for as the dinner offering."

Agatha's knitting group filed silently out of the café, waving goodbye to me as they went. Agatha came and joined us at the grill's counter.

"The soup sounds nice. Perfect for a cold, winter's day," he said as Agatha slid onto the seat next to him. The newcomer glanced over at Agatha and then did a double-take, his smile growing with obvious interest.

Agatha extended her hand in the way that a queen might. "It's nice to meet you."

"I assure you, the pleasure's all mine. My name's Conrad Holt," he said as he took her offered hand.

"Agatha Rayans," Agatha offered in kind. The air between them practically sizzled.

Zoey and I looked at each other again, then I went and got Conrad a bowl of soup with a freshly toasted crostini. I also got Agatha a fresh cup of hot cocoa.

"So you drove up all the way from Florida," Agatha said.

"I did. I knew I could have flown, but I've always enjoyed the road."

"And what brings you to town?" I asked.

"Mmm, sad business. A funeral of an old friend."

The hairs on the back of my neck stood up. "I'm so sorry. Might I ask who the old friend was? Maybe I knew them." I didn't want to offer up Mike's name. If that's who Conrad was here to see, I wanted to hear his name unprompted from Conrad's mouth.

"Mike Pratt. We went to college together."

I felt as though the heavens had opened up and beamed me down a present. No wonder Agatha was so attracted to him. He was an angel.

"You and Mike were close friends?" I asked. I did my best to keep the overenthusiasm I was feeling out of my voice. I didn't want Conrad to clam up because I'd done or said something to make him wary of me.

"Not as close as we once were," Conrad said. "We were roommates in college. Good friends. You know, the usual. Late nights at the bar followed by studying all night." He laughed. "Those were good times."

"Did you lose touch?" Zoey asked, prompting him for more information.

"For a time, then we reconnected over Facebook ohhhh... maybe ten years ago."

I didn't want to be insensitive, but I

needed to ask. “Do you, um, know anything about how he died?”

Conrad nodded his head, his expression somber. “I do. Sad business, that.” The nodding shifted into a head shake. “What a way to go.”

“Do you have any idea who might have done it?” Zoey asked.

“Done it?” Conrad asked with surprise. “It was an accident. His scarf. It got caught in his shredder.”

Zoey, Agatha and I all took turns looking at each other. Finally, Agatha covered one of Conrad’s hands with her own. “The police are looking into Mike’s death as a homicide.”

Conrad’s mouth fell open and his shoulders slumped. “A homicide. Murder? They think he was murdered? Who would do such a thing?”

“We were kind of hoping that you could shine some light on that question,” I said.

Conrad’s gaze drifted around the room as if searching through his memory banks. Finally, he shook his head. “I’ve got nothing. Mike was a nice guy. Got along with everybody."

The Mike that Conrad had known was definitely not the Mike that Susie had known.

"Do you know if he had a girlfriend?" I asked.

Conrad snorted and smiled. "That man had a revolving door of ladies in his life, at least so far as I could tell. Here," he said, pulling out his cell phone. "I've got pictures he sent me of his vacations. This one was of him and a lady named, um"—he tapped the phone's screen with his finger—"Jessica. This one was Jessica." She was a Catherine-Zeta Jones lookalike in a black string bikini lounging on the deck of what looked like an enormous yacht. No one else was in sight other than Mike. So most likely, it was a private yacht and not a group cruise.

Conrad swiped his finger across his phone's face. "This one is of him in the Alps on a skiing trip." Again, there was with an extraordinarily beautiful woman by his side. If Halle Berry and Sophia

Loren somehow managed to have a baby together, the woman in the picture could have been her. The lavish vacations went on for several more pictures, and each picture sported a different beautiful woman.

"So many different beautiful women," Agatha said.

"Yet not one of them have anything on my present company," Conrad said. He didn't single anyone out with his words, but his gaze was locked on Agatha.

"Aren't you the charming one?" Agatha said with the hint of a giggle in her voice.

Zoey and I looked at each other, then back at the pair. Agatha was at least twenty-five years older than Conrad, but their chemistry and connection was undeniable.

"I'd love to learn more about this charming little burg that I'm in," Conrad said. "Possibly you could keep me company and tell me all about it?"

"I'd love to," was Agatha's reply as she

guided her hand into his in a genteel fashion as she slipped off the tall stool.

The two retired to one of the booths lining the café's outer wall. Agatha sat on one side and Conrad sat on the other, but they leaned toward each other like a couple of high school kids out on their first date, both starry-eyed for the other one.

"He's scamming her," Zoey said in a deadpan voice as soon as the two got settled out of earshot.

"Nooo," I disagreed. "They're really into each other."

"Nope, he's scamming her, and I'm going to prove it."

Zoey was making me nervous, and I took a step away. Her eyes looked ready to shoot laser beams at Conrad.

"What are you planning on doing?" I asked. Angering Zoey was a little like angering the guy who knew the nuclear launch codes. What they *could* do was a lot.

"I'm going to expose him for the

conniving, scheming, manipulative, lying scab that he is."

"Gonna find dirt on the internet?"

"Yep."

"While you're doing that, think you could find out what properties Mike owned and maybe how much he was worth?"

"Yep, the man is going down."

"Mike?" He was going down. Six feet under as of tomorrow.

"Nope. Conrad."

CHAPTER 10

It was Friday morning before dawn, and I was starting the day with a steaming hot bath. I was tired of bone-chilling showers that felt like I was standing under a waterfall of ice cubes. It had taken pot after pot of hot water heated up on the stove, but I finally got the tub full enough to immerse myself. It was heaven.

I had a bear claw tub. The sides were high, and the top rim was curled. There, Sage sat, watching me. She slow-blinked her green-gold eyes and occasionally reached a paw out into space as if she could stretch it across the water's surface to touch my face. She had considered trying to walk across the water, but a few pats of the wet stuff had convinced her not to try. For whatever reason, she didn't simply walk along the tub's curving edge until she reached where I was resting my head, and in the end she did what I was doing. She bathed her smoky tortoiseshell fur with long licks of her tongue. Well, I used a washcloth, but the effect was the same.

When we arrived downstairs in the kitchen, the café was dark and cold. Too cold. With the boiler out, it seemed as if the very bones of the building had slowly lost all of their stored up heat until there was only the harsh absence of warmth.

Brenda wasn't going to be here today. It was just me and Sage. I got every burner of the six-burner stove lit and topped them with pots of hot water. I got the two ovens heating up as well, then I headed out into the café to shovel ash out of the Cozy Corner's wood stove and get a crackling fire going. Next, I fired up the griddle-style grill and topped it with several pots of water.

Even with all that work, the café hadn't done a thing to warm up. I could still see the mist of my breath in front of my face.

I heard a tap at the café's locked front door and felt a sudden surge of hope and worry about the homeless people that Zoey and I had met in the park near Mike's house. Had they been outside all night? Suffering the cold and waiting for me to show up?

I rushed to the front door, but the person standing on the other side was dressed from head to toe in thickly padded winter gear. He even had a ski mask over his mouth. His shoulders were broad and he was a head and a half taller than me.

My hand went to the door's lock, but my fingers didn't turn the latch that would give him entrance. Was he here to kill me? Rob me? Was he here for an early breakfast?

The man pulled the front of his ski mask down until it caught below his chin. "My name is Angus Wheeler," he yelled through the door. "I do construction. Joel said you were needing a heater." He shifted to the side and looked behind himself. I looked with him and saw a device that looked as though it belonged on a jet airplane as an engine.

Joel.

Him saying Joel's name was like saying the magic words open sesame. I popped the lock and pushed open the door. Angus wheeled the white, wheel-mounted, cylindrical device in. It was at least four feet long.

"Sorry. Didn't mean to scare you," Angus said.

"Oh, no worries." A total lie. There had been worries. "You know Joel?" I prompted him. I needed a bit more information before I could feel at ease in this situation.

"Oh, yeah. We go way back. Played football together in high school. I do construction now, and we use these blowers to keep construction sites warm during cold weather. He said you were in need of one and asked if I could drop by a loaner."

I gasped my delight and surprise, which resulted in a billowing cloud of cold mist.

"I'll take that as a yes," he laughed.

He got the thing plugged into a wall socket near the entryway into the grill and kitchen. He then rolled it several feet away from the wall and pointed the business end of its cigar shape away from everything. He flipped a switch. There was the tiniest of whirring sounds, and then WOOSH! The jet engine came to life, spewing instant heat out its front.

I moved to stand several feet in front of it, enjoying the push of warm air it blew toward me. But it was very loud.

"This is amazing!" I yelled over the sound of the heater.

"Give it fifteen or twenty minutes, and it will have this whole place heated up to a comfortable temperature," he yelled back. He demonstrated a knob on its side that could be used to cycle the thing on and off with the help of a built-in thermostat.

Angus left, and as the café heated up, I marveled at how Joel had yet again managed to take care of me. He was so low-key in his approach. He never made a fuss over what he did for me, and he never made helping me about creating a situation to garner congratulations for himself.

That earlier image of me sitting on the Cozy Corner's loveseat with one of my suitors was quickly coming into focus with Joel by my side.

Leaving the heater to do its work, I headed back into the kitchen. I needed to get to cooking… something.

I closed my eyes and imagined what would be a good breakfast on a cold winter's morning. I frowned. My mind was a blank.

I got out my phone and surfed Google for ideas. And then, I hit on a good one.

"Biscuits and gravy!" I whispered. I felt like I'd found the holy grail. I did some Googling just to be sure. Yep, it was definitely known as a southern dish.

I looked up some recipes. I had all of the ingredients, but I was completely unsure of my ability to pull it off.

"Won't know until I try," I said to Sage. She was staying way clear of the loud blower set up in the body of the café. She peeked around the corner a couple of times at it only to sit back down, look at me and meow.

"I know, sweetie. It is pretty intimidating." But I could already feel a difference in the café's warmth. I turned off the stove, ovens, and grill, then emptied the pots of water, dried them and put them away.

Next I laid out all the ingredients to make homemade biscuits. Just like on all the cooking shows I'd taken to watching, I measured out all of my ingredients in advance and put each ingredient in its own little bowl. I even put Post-It notes on the bowls to label what they were.

It took me far longer than I was sure it had taken anybody ever to make homemade biscuits. Pulling a tray out of the oven, I held my breath as I eyed the many golden mounds. Then, picking one up, I pulled at its top to split it in half. I breathed deep its steamy goodness, and my eyes rolled back in my head.

I turned to Sage. "I did it! I really did it!" I took a bite. It was delicious! I slathered it with butter and took another bite. My hand slapped the countertop as I chewed. It was the only thing that I knew to do with the overwhelming pleasure of just how good that biscuit was.

While the biscuits had been in the oven, I'd started on the gravy. I'd already thrown two batches out and was on my third batch, but I was feeling good about this one. I even had some bacon cooked up good and crispy.

"Anybody here?" I heard a man's voice call. Even over the noise of the loud, blowing heater, I recognized the voice as Brad's.

I rushed out into the café to find him kneeling next to the jet engine contraption. I leaned down next to him to turn its temperature dial down, and the loud, hard-blowing heater powered off.

"Where'd you get this thing?"

"Joel arranged it. A guy dropped it off this morning."

"Joel..." Brad said, but he didn't say it in a nice way. He said it more in a Lex-Luthor-you-are-my-nemesis kind of way.

"Hey," I said and tapped Brad on the shoulder. "I've got a surprise for you. Biscuits and gravy."

"Really? No kidding me, now. You're not teasing? Real biscuits and real gravy. Not that stuff out of a jar." Brad stood up.

"Real biscuits. Real sausage gravy. Everything from scratch. I've even got bacon made, and I can make some scrambled eggs, too." It was my single best solo accomplishment.

Brad was smiling from ear to ear, and he tucked his thumbs into his uniform's belt. "Joel might've gotten you a snazzy heater, but I know who you like."

I laughed and slapped him on his arm with the back of my hand. "You sit. I'll get a breakfast plate made up for you."

"I'll get the coffee made while you do that."

I was sure that Brad sprinkled pixie dust in the coffee every time he made it. It always turned out better than mine.

Between the two of us, we got him set up for a breakfast fit for a southern king. When I put the plate in front of him, he said, "No, no. Get you a plate and eat with me. I'll wait."

I was surprised. I didn't know quite what to do with myself. I'd made breakfast or lunch for Brad a few dozen times now. He was my most faithful early morning customer. He'd suffered through every concoction imaginable and had still come back the next day. And the day after that. And the day after that.

Like lightning striking out of the blue, everything I'd thought I'd known changed. While it was true that Joel had quietly been there for me when I'd needed him, doing things to help my life go smoother, Brad had been walking the marathon. He'd been here every day that the café had been open. He'd eaten everything I put in front of him. He'd come back time and time again, and I knew that it wasn't for the food. It was for me.

That image of me sitting on the couch with Joel morphed. Instead of Joel, Brad was sitting right next to me. Settled in. Ready to stay a while.

"I'll be right back," I said, feeling slightly humbled and a little shy.

I ran back into the kitchen and scrambled up a couple of eggs. Loading a plate with a few slices of bacon, then I pulled one of my beautiful biscuits apart before ladling creamy sausage gravy over it.

As promised, Brad was waiting on me when I got back to him. He hadn't eaten anything yet.

Along with my plate of food, I'd brought back with me a small plate of extra biscuits and some strawberry jam I'd found in the walk-in cooler.

Walking around to the customer side of the grill's counter, I sat down on the stool next to Brad's. That's when he slid a cup of coffee over to me.

"Made you a cup," he said.

I looked at the coffee, then I looked at him. Without giving myself the chance to over think it, I leaned over and gave Brad a kiss on the cheek.

Brad didn't say anything. He just smiled down at his plate as he dug in. He groaned as soon as he took his first bite of biscuit. "Oh my God. Can you make this tomorrow? Can you make this every day—for the rest of your life?"

I laughed. "I'm not sure about every day, but I can promise to make it at least once a week."

"I'll be here!"

Yes, he will, I thought as I watched him eat. *He really will.*

CHAPTER 11

Brad had long since gone, along with a few others who had dropped in for breakfast. Everybody raved over the biscuits and gravy, and I made a note in my little notebook to make it a signature dish for the café.

Every time the café emptied out of all its customers, I cranked the heater up and let it blow hot air throughout the space. As soon as a customer walked in, I turned it off. Nobody complained.

It was after ten by the time Zoey walked in. She was dressed in a thickly padded parka and fishnet stockings atop boots that looked as though they belonged on a construction site with

Angus. Her thick black hair was in an extra messy half-updo—that is to say that the upper half was pulled into a messy bun near the nape of her neck and the rest was left to fly wild.

I could take all of that in stride. It wasn't that I'd seen her in that outfit before, but it was Zoey-esque, nonetheless. What I was surprised to see—and that I hadn't seen before—was a pair of Jackie-O sunglasses that covered up most of Zoey's face. They were the kind often worn by women trying to hide a black eye.

Zoey stomped her way over to the grill's counter, plopped down on top of one of the stools and slouched.

"Want some coffee?" I asked.

"Did you make it?" she mumbled.

Ouch. "No, Brad made a double pot this morning."

"Then, yes."

I didn't know what to think. I'd never known Zoey to be mean, at least not to me and not without provocation.

Giving Zoey the benefit of the doubt

and not negatively reacting to her surliness, I quietly got her a cup of coffee and slid the chilled silver container of organic cream and the little spoon pot of sugar over to her. She didn't perk up as she loaded up her coffee with the mix she liked. She stayed slouched with her neck and chin dropped forward.

Finally, feeling bold, I reached across the counter, and pinched the center piece of her sunglasses. Gently, I lifted them away from her face.

Phew. No black eye, at least not one that heavy eyeliner didn't give her. Her eyes were bloodshot, though, kind of like she'd been awake all night. Staring unblinking at her computer screens.

"Want some biscuits and gravy?"

"No."

"Jelly and biscuits, or honey and butter on a biscuit?"

"No."

I had to think. Zoey was in a curmudgeon's mood. That's when it came to me. Without saying a word, I left Zoey there and ran upstairs to my apartment. I was back two minutes later. I had just the thing to brighten her up. I poured a tall glass of cold milk and presented Zoey with a plate of Oreo cookies.

She smiled. Finally. It was a small one. But I saw it, I swear.

I left her to eat her cookies and went and fixed her a plate of biscuits, gravy, bacon and eggs. I even drew a smiley face with ketchup on top of the eggs. She'd said she didn't want any biscuits and gravy, but I was trusting the cookies to act as a primer to her appetite.

It worked. As soon as I got back and put the plate of food in front of her, she started eating. She sat up a little taller, and her head drooped a little less.

"This is good," she said, and I knew the crisis had passed. She was on her way to getting on top of whatever it was that had her feeling so grumpy.

I went to take care of my other customers. There were more this morning than usual, and I was pretty sure that the café was actually managing to operate in the black. Of course, it helped that I didn't have any paid staff working yet today. It was just me. But, that wouldn't last for long. Sweet Melanie, my waitress, was due in at any time. I'd pulled out a lasagna that Brenda had prepped and frozen for me. And I had a large bowl of tossed salad almost done. Everything would be ready to go for easy serving after Zoey and I left. Melanie would be able to handle taking care of customers all on her own.

Mike Pratt's funeral was today, and Zoey and I were going to go. Zoey had been wearing a black wraparound dress with white polka dots underneath her parka. As for me, my jeans, t-shirt and cardigan would have to be changed out for some more funeral appropriate attire.

Zoey had her plate half cleared by the time I got back to her.

"Okay, it's time. What gives?" I asked. I saw a flash of surliness return to Zoey's eyes, but it was gone just as fast.

"I was up all night researching fat face."

"Come again? Researching who?"

"Fat face. Conrad. That's what I'm calling him."

Conrad didn't even have a fat face. I didn't know where Zoey's hostility was coming from.

"I couldn't believe how Agatha swooned for him," she went on. "She's old enough to know better. She's older than any of us. Why wouldn't she know better?"

"Know better about what?"

Zoey looked at me like I'd just asked her if she thought it was okay if I drank poison.

"That all men are scum!" Zoey blurted.

Ohhhhh... Things were starting to make sense. Zoey's heart had been put in a blender and then blowtorched. She'd been through so much.

I leaned on my forearms atop the counter. "So what kind of scummy things did you find out about Conrad?"

"Nothing," she said, the surliness back. She stabbed at her breakfast and ate it angrily, like it had somehow wronged her. "He's from Florida.

Widower of a woman he was married to for over thirty years. Grown kids that are close to him. Adoring grandfather. Sat by his wife's side through a long illness. Financially comfortable. No embezzling. No laundering. No out of control gambling, drinking, or drug habits. Nothing."

She stabbed at the biscuit so hard that her fork clinked against the plate. She sounded very unhappy that she hadn't been able to dig up any dirt on Agatha's starry-eyed suitor, Conrad.

She shook her fork at me. "All men are scum. I just have to find out how this one is scum."

I took a beat to let her words rest and to let their echoes vacate the quiet, empty space between us. "And Brad, is he scum, too? Or Joel? Or Jack?" It was true that Brad had taken a turn at investigating both me and Zoey for murder, but I didn't think that him doing his best to do his job should relegate him to the category of scum.

"They're not men," Zoey answered

scornfully. "They're just them. They don't count."

"I'm not sure Jack's wife would agree," I said with a playful chuckle. It won me a smile from Zoey.

"I guess not," she conceded.

I started absentmindedly wiping the countertop with a cleaning cloth, dividing my attention between Zoey and my work. I wanted to nudge an idea at Zoey, not shove it down her throat. People resisted when you tried to force an idea on them. "Maybe Conrad's like Jack?" I finally said.

Zoey scowled, clearly not ready to bestow upon Conrad the same respect she had for Jack.

I left her to her stewing and took care of some more customers. Then, Melanie made it in, and I brought her up to speed on the work that was ahead of her.

When I made it back to Zoey, I asked, "Were you able to find out anything about what properties Mike owned?"

Zoey shook her head. "I tapped into the County Clerk's records, but they only go back to 1988. Mike most likely bought his properties before that and the paper documents haven't been converted over to the digital storage yet."

"Digital storage?"

"Yeah, they haven't been recorded in the office's online database."

"So we'll have to go there in person?"

"Not me," Zoey said. "I can handle only so much human contact. People are too weird." She narrowed her eyes. "Especially in contained, isolated groups like government offices. They're the worst. I vote that we go talk to Mike's ex, what's-her-name."

"Emily?"

"Yeah, her."

We didn't have a last name. "Think she'll be at Mike's funeral?"

Zoey shrugged. "Who knows? Maybe we'll get lucky."

CHAPTER 12

The old Victorian house that was being used as a funeral home sat forty feet off the road. A sign on the lawn announced it as the Williamson Funeral Home. I guessed there was parking behind it, but Zoey had opted to park on the street. That left us with a forty foot walk up a narrow concrete walkway to the funeral home's front door.

When we stepped inside, we were out of the harsh cold, but that was the only improvement. Inside, the home was chilly and the air was stale. It smelled like the inside of a refrigerator after the fans stopped working. Everything was dead about the home, figuratively and literally.

"Good afternoon. Thank you for coming. Can I take your coats?" asked a man with a deep baritone voice that almost seemed to echo all on its own without any help from its surroundings. His nose was so large and so hooked that it could have almost been used to pop the top off of soda bottles. He was tall, lanky, and skeleton thin. His skin wasn't white in the way most Caucasians were white—there was a complete absence of color. He was the neon of white. Hard to even look at without having to blink repeatedly from the strain of reflective glare.

"I'll take those," said another man stepping up to stand next to the first. His skin was a warm, dark brown and his smile was so big and glamorous that it could have stopped a mugger mid-wallet reach. His body was lithe, lean and graceful. Draping Zoey's parka and my princess coat over his arm, he turned to the tall man and looked up at him from beneath eyelashes that Elizabeth Taylor would have envied. "I've set the refreshments out."

"Thank you, Jasper," the first man said without looking at him.

Jasper's eager smile turned into a scowl, apparently not pleased with the response. Turning on his heel, he headed on his way, his back rigid and his chin held high.

"I apologize for my partner's exuberance," the tall man said. "Jasper does not yet grasp the required decorum at these functions. My name is Samuel Gringot. Please let me know if you need anything."

He started to turn away, but Zoey's raised finger and her utterance of, "Uh," stopped him.

"Yes?" he said, turning back around and giving Zoey his full attention. With his hands clasped behind his back, there was a curved lean forward to his stance that made him look as though was not just taller than us but that he was towering over us. It was unnerving, to say the least.

"When you say partner..." Zoey's

voice trailed off. It sounded as though she was trying to ask something without being so blatant as to actually ask it.

"Yes. Times are changing, aren't they? I should have said 'husband.'"

I did not see that coming. Samuel looked like death dug up out of the ground two weeks after the fact. Jasper looked as though he would be the life of the party. Above ground. Among the land of the breathing.

I guessed it was true. Opposites did attract.

Samuel went on his way, and I did my best to suppress the urge to strangle Zoey for embarrassing me. Then the thought of strangling her embarrassed me even more, given the reason for Mike's funeral.

We made our way down the hallway to a large, open parlor. There was a large framed picture of Mike beside an open casket. Inside, Mike was dressed in an expensive suit. He was not wearing a tie or even a bow tie. Gorgeous yet understated flowers adorned the casket on top and at both ends. Elegant but not festive.

The rest of the room was filled with fold-out chairs.

"There's almost nobody here," I whispered to Zoey, despite the fact that I was stating the obvious. Almost all the chairs were empty. "Are we early?"

"Nope. On time."

There were a couple of small groups of three people gathered, talking low amongst themselves. They were standing, and they were dressed in clothes one might wear to go out to dinner. They weren't exactly festive, but they certainly weren't dark.

There was one woman sitting, and she was alone. She was also crying. And she was dressed from head to toe in black.

"Emily?" I said.

"Maybe."

I went one way and Zoey went the other. Together, we sat down on either side of the crying woman. I guessed her to be in her mid to late 40s. She was a little plump and her age was starting to catch up to her. She looked tired, and her tears looked genuine.

"I'm sorry for your loss," I said.

The woman sniffed and dabbed at her eyes with a shaky hand. She wasn't wearing a wedding ring.

"Emily?" Zoey said.

The woman looked at her. "Who? No." She dabbed at her eyes some more. "Who are you?" Even though we were sitting on either side of her, she managed to address the question to both of us.

"My name is Kylie Berry, and this is Zoey Jin." I paused, unsure of what to say next. We weren't friends with Mike. I'd never even met him when he was alive. And on the day that he'd died, Zoey and I had been on our way to his place to blackmail him. That wasn't much of an opener to gain the trust of someone clearly grieving his passing.

"We're looking into Mike's death," Zoey said.

The woman's bloodshot eyes opened wide and an expression I could only describe as hope filled her face. "You are?"

Honesty worked. Who knew? I made a mental note to myself to consider trying it first next time instead of doing my best to think up a handy dandy lie.

"Yes, we are," Zoey said. "May we ask what your relationship to Mike Pratt was?"

She sniffed again. "He was my brother."

Jackpot! If I could have done a high-five with Zoey above the woman's head without being noticed, I would have.

Zoey continued with her interrogative questions. "And what is your name?"

"Claudia Abramson. Abramson was my married name. Widowed."

"Do you know of anyone who may have wanted to do Mike harm?" Zoey asked.

Claudia slumped in her chair as her eyes drifted around the floor in front of her. Finally she shook her head. "Mike and me haven't been very close for a long time now," she said with a note of apology in her voice.

"Did you used to be close?" I asked.

"He was about ten years older than me, so we didn't really do a lot of growing up together, but I'd thought we were pretty close."

"When did that change?" I asked.

Her face grew long as a resigned sadness settled in. "When I asked him for money."

Ohhh... Mike did seem to be rather fond of his money.

"We'd wanted to buy a house," she went on, "but the down payment was more than we could do. After I asked him for help, things were never the same between us again."

"I'm sorry," I said, and I meant it. I didn't think much of Mike, but his sister had genuinely seemed to care about him. When he'd died, she'd lost someone she had held dear.

"Can you tell us anything about Conrad Holt?" Zoey asked.

"Conrad Holt..." Claudia paused in thought. "I don't know who that is."

"Did you know any of Mike's friends from high school or college?"

She shook her head. "No, not really. There was so much age between us.

When he was in high school, I was still very young. And he never brought any friends home from college."

Zoey's lips tightened and her eyes narrowed. Zoey had struck out on digging any dirt up on Conrad again, and I could see that it wasn't sitting well with her.

"How did Mike get so much money?" I asked, taking over the questioning.

"He won the lottery. Won millions."

That was a lot of money. I hadn't realized it had been so much.

"Do you know who will inherit?" I asked.

"I don't know, but not me."

"Why not you?"

She shrugged. "When he helped me with the down payment of the house, he told me then that I'd never get another dollar from him. Said I was on my own and to never ask for help again." She didn't sound bitter. She looked reflective. "He wasn't always like that," she said. "He'd take me for ice cream cones when I was a kid or bring me back a present when he'd come back from college. He'd always been generous with me back when he didn't have hardly anything to be generous with."

"What changed that? What made him stop wanting to be generous?"

"After he won the lottery, he had a bunch of girlfriends. Every time he called home, he'd mention a new girlfriend. Always a different one. This went on for maybe five years. Over and over, he'd say, 'this is the one,' only to end up having a different girlfriend a few weeks later."

"I don't understand," I said. "How would that change him from a person who had been generous to someone who wasn't generous?"

"He told me later that all those girls had milked him to see how much they could get out of him with expensive presents and trips and then they'd dumped him. Every single one. It made him not trust anyone. After that he was always looking for how others were trying to play him. He didn't trust anyone." She rubbed at her chest with her fingertips as if to rub some pain away. "I hate that he lumped me together with all of them, that he thought that I wanted to take advantage of him and didn't care about him."

"And you're sure he didn't leave you anything?" I asked.

"Positive. He wouldn't have. He just wouldn't."

"So someone else is due to inherit," Zoey said, latching onto the information with both hands. "Maybe a friend. Maybe someone he knew in school." She wasn't calling Conrad out by name, but she might as well have written it in permanent ink across her forehead.

"Claudia, do you know any of the other people here?" I asked.

She took a moment to scan the room before shaking her head.

Among those in attendance, Conrad was nowhere in sight. Neither was Susie, but that didn't surprise me. Even if Susie didn't kill Mike, they weren't on the best of terms. I wondered if any of the others in attendance might be some of his other renters.

"And do you know anyone named Emily?" I asked. I hoped that she could give us a clue about the woman Mike had considered marrying. Without a last name, she would be hard to track down.

Claudia thought, then her face lit up. "Oh! My son's first grade teacher had been named Emily."

"How long ago was your son in first grade?" Zoey asked.

"About eighteen years ago."

"Did Mike ever meet her?" I asked.

"No, not that I know of."

The Emily we were looking for was engaged to Mike about five years ago. I was pretty sure that Claudia's son's first grade teacher and Mike's fiancé were not one in the same, especially since they probably had never met.

Zoey and I excused ourselves from Claudia and meandered around the room. We got names when we could, as well as affiliations. One clear-eyed mourner was a representative from the bank. Another was Mike's stockbroker. Then there was Mike's accountant. Everybody in attendance seemed to have done work for Mike and Mike's money. Nobody knew about his will or who was going to be executing his will. Nobody was a personal, close friend.

A throat cleared and we all turned our attention to the front of the room. A short man with a Bible in his hands was standing a few feet away from Mike's casket.

Everyone standing, Zoey and myself included, found a chair. That left ten chairs full and what looked like another thirty-five chairs empty. It was a modest and sad turnout.

"Dearly beloved, we are gathered here today," the man at the front began, then stopped when there was the sound of more attendees coming down the hall. To my astonishment, in walked Derek, Winnie, Patty, and Manny—the homeless people who had been living in the park next to Mike's house. They were some of the few people to who Mike had shown kindness, so I didn't know why I was so surprised that they would come to pay their last respects.

"Dearly beloved," the preacher began again, but once more stopped upon the entrance of yet another newcomer. It was Conrad. He didn't spot us. He simply took a seat in the front row, and the preacher continued.

"That's Conrad. Are you sure you don't know him?" Zoey whispered to Claudia by twisting around in her seat.

Claudia studied Conrad, then shook her head. "No."

CHAPTER 13

Mike's funeral had been short and filled with generalities. There hadn't been anything specific about it. It was clear that the preacher hadn't known Mike, and no one in attendance had stood up to reminisce about his life. It had been a cold, sterile event, and it made me think that the funeral itself had probably not been much different than the days he'd spent in the morgue, waiting for his final farewell.

"Where to next?" Zoey asked when we were back in the car.

"Let's go see Susie. She hadn't reopened her shop the last time I talked her, but maybe we'll get lucky. Maybe she'll know who Emily is or maybe she'll know of someone else who would know who Emily is."

When we reached the road where Susie's shop was, not only was Susie's shop open, but all the other little shops on both sides of the road were open as well. Agatha had said that Mike had bought up the store fronts on both sides of the road. If that were true, then that meant that it was business as usual for all of Mike's renters. It was yet another testimony to the lack of positive impact that Mike had had on the people in his life. No one was actively trying to remember him or celebrate his life. He was like a stone that gets thrown into a pond. The stone sinks but doesn't make a hole. That water simply fills in above it so that a person would never know it had even been there.

It made me wonder: if I were to die at this point in my life, would my disappearance go unnoticed as well? Would there be anyone who would feel my absence?

"We're here," Zoe said, putting the car in park and turning off the engine.

Looking over at her, I realized that she was the person who would miss me. In fact, she was *my* person. My go-to person. My where-the-heck-are-you person anytime anything went good or bad in my life. Thelma and Louise. Lucy and Ethel. Romy and Michelle. It had happened so fast that I wasn't even sure when it had happened. But it had. And because of that—because of her—no matter what, I knew that I'd be missed if something happened to me. Not just mourned, but missed.

"What?" Zoey asked, narrowing her eyes suspiciously. I guess that I'd stared at her a little too long as I marveled over what our friendship had grown into. Zoey wiped at her face. "I got a booger on my nose or something?"

"Just a small one," I teased. I waved my finger at her face near the end of her nose. "Right here."

Zoey rubbed at her nose.

"Ewww," I said, making face. "You just smeared it."

Zoey yanked the rearview mirror in

her direction, saw that her face was clean, then smacked me on the arm. "Payback's a b—"

"Bucket of chicken? Please say it's a bucket of chicken." There wasn't a reception after the funeral—which meant no food—and I was hungry.

"How are you so skinny?" Zoey asked. "I've never seen anybody as small as you eat so much."

"Hazards of the trade," I shot back. "I gotta taste the food to know if it's any good."

"I'm amazed your taste buds still work after torturing them with your cooking. You need new taste buds… attached to a chef. A really cute chef who used to be a male stripper and who like to cook in only an apron."

"Hey! I run a family-friendly business. He has to at least wear boxers."

We got out of the car and headed toward *Susie's Clip & Dye*. The "Open" sign was flipped outward. Inside we found Susie with a client. Susie's eyes were shiny and red-rimmed, and her hand shook as she held the tips of the woman's hair between her fingers in preparation to cut.

"Hi," I said. I instantly regretted not coming with something in hand, something like chocolate muffins or a to-go order of lasagna from the café. Comfort food. Susie looked terrible. She looked like she could use a little chicken soup for the soul. "I know you're with a client, but do you have a minute?"

"Sure," she said. If anything, Susie looked relieved for the interruption.

We followed her to the back of her shop and through a door that led to a little room. Every inch of wall was lined with shelves, and all the shelves were packed full of hair care product. The air had a slight chemical scent, and I guessed it was from the hastily rinsed bowls containing hair dye mixture in the small room's utility sink.

Susie sat down on a low step stool. Her knees were high and pressed together and her feet were splayed far apart. She slouched, and I wouldn't have been surprised if a cigarette had magically materialized in her hand. She looked like she needed one.

"I was a little surprised to see you open today," I said. She did not look together enough to be here.

"Betty across the street has been trying to steal my customers ever since I opened shop here. She's such a... a... whatever you can think of that's bad, she's worse. I had to come in or I'd have no clients left by the time this all gets sorted."

"How are things going?"

"Not good." She ran a shaky hand through her glossy brown hair. "They had me in for questioning for eight hours yesterday. Eight hours straight!" Even her voice shook, and it sounded as worn thin as she looked.

"When's that last time you slept?" I asked on a hunch.

"Almost none at all, not since Mr. Pratt got killed." She swiped a tear away from her cheek. "I keep having nightmares. I keep seeing him die. His hand reaching out, all desperate and scared."

It was quite the image, and I couldn't help wonder if it were a memory rather than a product of her imagination.

"Is that the way it happened?" I asked.

"The way what happened?" Susie asked.

"Is that how Mr. Pratt looked as he died?"

Susie turned instantly indignant. "How the heck would I know? You think I did it, don't you? Just like everybody else."

I didn't know what to say to that. She was certainly top of the list, but we were doing the best we could to find a person to replace her as suspect number one.

"Do you know anyone named Emily?" Zoey asked with a calm voice. It helped to diffuse the sudden anger that had filled the room.

"Emily? What about her?"

Bingo!

"We had some questions," Zoey answered.

Susie's wounded, accusatory gaze cut

to me. "You're investigating this, aren't you? Even after I told you to stay out?"

I knelt down so that I could be more at eye level with Susie. I put a hand on her knee. "Is us not investigating helping you any?"

Susie closed her eyes, and a couple more tears slipped free. She shook her head no.

"So what's the harm in if we talk to people?"

Susie opened her eyes and pinned me with a stare full of so much fear that it was hard not to look away. "This is my life, Kylie. It's not a game. If you mess things up for the cops, if you get in the way, where does that leave me? What if the killer gets away because of something you do? You're amateurs, Kylie. Both of you. You got lucky solving those other two murders, but I don't want you taking those risks with my life. If you mess this up, it's me that goes away to prison. Not you. Me. I'd rather take my chances with the professionals."

"But Susie, the professionals think

that you did it. They're looking into every possible way to connect you to Mike Pratt's murder." It was honestly a guess. I was sure that I wasn't being fair to the police's investigative process. But it was Susie who they'd questioned for eight hours yesterday. That sounded like they were trying to get her to crack, trying to get her to confess. If that were true, they probably weren't considering any other possibilities.

Susie had been there the day that Mike had gotten killed. In fact, she'd been there twice, and she'd had a big argument with him because he'd been trying to ruin her financially. He'd also had her trapped in a contract that she wanted out of. He was even threatening a lawsuit. On top of all of that, her fingerprints were all over the murder weapon —the shredder.

Means. Motive. Opportunity. Susie had them all. I couldn't blame the police for making her the focus of their investigation. Everything was pointing to her.

"But I didn't do it," Susie said,

sounding like a lost little girl. "I'm innocent."

"Then let us help the police see that," I said. "Let us help you."

Susie didn't seem convinced. Her lips were pinched tightly together.

It was Zoey's turn to press again. "Where can we find Emily?"

Silence hung in the air for so long that I almost shattered it by saying that she knew where to find us if she decided to talk. But then she cracked. She gave us what we needed.

"Emily owns the bath and candle shop down the street, but I don't know why you want to talk to her. I don't think she even rented her space from him."

"Thanks, Susie," I said, standing up in preparation to go.

Susie grabbed my hand. "Don't screw this up for me, Kylie. I don't want to go to jail."

CHAPTER 14

One of the biggest differences between Camden Falls and Chicago was that in Camden Falls everybody drives everywhere. There is no bus. There is no train. There is no public transportation beyond taxis and services like Uber. And if a person was to decide to walk, they'd do so at their own peril. Once you got off of Main Street, none of the roads had shoulders or sidewalks. There was road and then there was dirt and grass—if you were lucky. Sometimes there was road and then there was air from where the ground would suddenly drop away from the side of the road by ten feet or more. No guard rail.

So instead of walking just down the street to Emily's store, *Scented Delights,* we drove. This time there was a small parking lot, and we parked in front of the store and headed in.

As soon as we opened the door to the little shop, a wall of scents washed over us. Instead of being overwhelming, though, it was nice. I could pick out cucumber, melon, lavender, pumpkin, pine, and vanilla. There were other scents, too, but they were lost to me, hidden among the others.

"Thank you. Come again," the woman at the cash register told a customer as she handed over a bag made heavy with its contents. I guessed her to be in her mid to late thirties. She was taller than either Zoey or me, but I wouldn't call her tall. She was slender but not skinny, and she had a pleasant and inviting face. She looked like the type of person you'd feel comfortable striking up a conversation with in the checkout lane of a store. She had a button nose, wore round, hippie-style glasses, and had dimples. But the feature that stood out to me the most was her thick black hair. The cut was different than the picture of the woman who was on vacation with Mike, but it could definitely be her.

I was sure that this Emily was the same Emily who Mike was rumored to have been in a serious relationship with.

Zoey and I looked around while the store's only other remaining customer finished shopping. As I looked around, I really hoped that Emily was not Mike's murderer. Her shop was really cute! She had shelves that spanned from countertop to ceiling, and they were all filled with things that I wanted to buy and take home. She had candles of every scent imaginable with all natural hemp, cotton or wood wicks. She also had bath salts, bath balms, lotions, and shampoos and conditioners. Most of the lotions and hair products were pre-scented, but you also had the option of coming up with custom scents.

I was absolutely in love. I wanted to come back here and spend every dime that I didn't have. I was tempted to give Zoey my purse so that she could guard my wallet. After all, I had a train engine-sized boiler to pay for.

"Thank you. Come again," the woman at the cash register said to the only other customer in the store. That person left, and then the cashier focused her attention on us. She came out from behind the checkout counter and headed our way.

"I don't believe I've seen you in here before," she said as she reached us. "I have a large line of items for relaxation and self-pampering, and I do custom gift baskets as well."

"It's a beautiful store," I said. *Please don't be the killer. Please don't be the killer. Please don't be the killer.* I wanted to buy at least one of everything she had, but I couldn't afford any of it. I'd have to wait. But if she was the killer, I wouldn't be able to get any of it... now or later. "Is this your store?"

"It is. I designed most of the products here. I'm Emily Winston."

Zoey spoke up next, which relieved

me. I was too smitten with all the beautiful candles and already daydreaming of sinking down into another hot bath with one of her bath bombs fizzing away.

"Will you have to relocate your store after the death of the property owner?" Zoey asked.

"The what?" Emily asked, looking a bit blindsided. "I own this property."

"Oh!" I said. It was time to prime the well and see if I got anything out of it. "It was our understanding that Mike Pratt owned this property."

"No, I purchased the property from Mike a few years ago."

Yay! We'd managed to establish a connection between Mike and this particular Emily. Now to see if she was the Emily who had been involved with Mike. "Was that before your relationship with Mike ended?" I asked.

Emily looked from me to Zoey and back, then crossed her arms over her chest. "Who are you? What's this about? I bought this property. I'm the deed holder, and I can prove it."

Shucks. She'd gone on the defensive without giving us any new information.

"We believe you," I said, hoping to soothe her sudden distrust of us. "We're friends with Susie up the street. She runs *Susie's Clip & Dye*. We know that Mike owned most of the property on both sides of the road. We'd just assumed that this was part of it."

"That still doesn't tell me who you are or why you're here."

I hadn't managed to put her at ease at all.

"We're looking into Mike's death," Zoey said, and I wished she hadn't. We still needed to talk to Mike's other tenants, and I didn't want word about what Zoey and I were doing to get out. If the killer found out, knowing that we were coming would give them time to work on their story and cover their tracks. Zoey and I didn't have the benefit of DNA evidence or even fingerprints. All we had in our bag of tricks was talking to people and hoping they revealed a tidbit of information that would get us one step closer to figuring out the truth.

"What's that got to do with me?" Emily asked. Her defensiveness hadn't eased, and it was time to bluff.

"You and Mike were a couple," I said. "You'd been in a serious relationship, and you went on vacation together. Yet you didn't even bother to go to his funeral."

Emily's arms dropped to her sides. "Our relationship ended almost three years ago."

I heard a note of guilt in her voice. I guessed it was because she didn't go to pay her final respects. "Why weren't you at the funeral?"

"It's none of your business."

"You're going to have more customers coming in sooner or later," Zoey said. "I'm guessing that you'd rather us not be here, asking you these questions when that happens."

Emily glanced at the door as her lips thinned with stress and disapproval. Zoey was right. Someone was bound to show up sooner or later. Talking about a dead body lying in the cold, hard ground would be a bit of a buzz kill for her feel-good business.

"Like I said, it's none of your business. Mike and I ended years ago."

"Then you won't mind talking to us about him," I said, "given that it won't be too upsetting for you."

The woman looked as though she wanted to call me a few choice words, but she chewed them around her mouth instead without letting any of them out. "What do you want to know?"

"Mike sold you this property. Why?" Zoey asked. "He hasn't sold off any of this other property."

Emily shrugged. "When our relationship ended, Mike was hurt. His pride was hurt. But, I think he was relieved, too."

"So you're the one who made the decision to end it?" I asked.

"I did. Mike had been there when I needed someone in my life. And, things were great at first. He was the sweetest guy… to me. But the more time I spent with him, it was like the mask would slip and I'd get a peek at the person behind it. He was horrible. He was so mean."

"But not to you?" I asked.

"No, not to me. He was always good to me. I, uh, never asked him for anything, you see. I think that might have been it. I finally noticed it in his dealings with others. He was great to people but as soon as they asked him for anything, he went from Dr. Jekyll to Mr. Hyde. He'd turn mean. Gleefully mean. It made him happy." Her face was scrunched like she'd just eaten something distasteful.

"So what happened between you?" Zoey asked.

Emily shrugged. "I gave his ring back. We didn't get married. And he let me buy this place from him as, I don't know, a breakup gift. I think that he cared what I thought about him and wanted me to think well of him and that that was why he let me buy this place. I've, uh, heard stories from some of his tenants. Not good stories. I know that he could be difficult."

Difficult. That was the nicest way I

could imagine ever describing Mike's opportunistic financial bullying.

It was Zoey's turn again. "Did you know that Mike was murdered?" As always, she managed to strike straight to the heart of the matter.

Emily leaned against the nearest counter, looking as though she needed the support. "I'd heard a rumor. I'd hoped it wasn't true."

"Any ideas who might have done it?"

Emily took a beat before answering. I could see her struggling with herself as to how much she wanted to say.

"If you know something that might shed light on what really happened to him, it might save somebody else from a similar fate. Kill once. What's to stop a person from killing again?"

That seemed to do it. Emily nodded. "We kept in touch after we broke up. Mostly from his doing. He'd call, drop by or text. He... I'm not sure he was well at the end."

"How so?" Maybe Mike was terminally ill and maybe faking his death had been his way of staying relevant in the land of the living for a little bit longer. And if someone got wrongly sent to prison for killing him, maybe that would make him all the happier. That thought made me wonder if Mike might be getting a permanent suntan in hell.

"He'd started complaining about things moving around on their own in his office or inside his house."

"What? You mean like a ghost?" Zoey asked.

"No, it wasn't happening in front of him. Things would go missing and then he'd find them a couple of days later in a different spot. His paranoia was through the roof. He'd started calling me more often, and would vent for hours."

"Were you afraid of him?" I asked on a hunch.

"Not at first, but here lately, it was like he'd lost touch with reality."

"Do you think he could have killed himself?" I asked.

"Oh! No, no… Not at all. No. It wasn't his way."

"What do you mean?" I asked.

"Mike liked himself too much to ever kill himself."

"But if he wasn't right in the head," Zoey prompted.

"Doesn't matter. He wouldn't do that. He was too afraid of someone else trying to do that. He was obsessed with the idea of someone poisoning him or breaking in and killing him for all his money. It's why he left all his money to charity, so no one would be able to gain from his death."

"He left it to charity? Are you sure?" If that were true, it would wipe an enormous possible motive for his murder off our list.

"I'm sure."

"Was that common knowledge?" Zoey asked, and her question made me want to kick myself. Of course. Mike's plans for his money didn't matter. The only thing that mattered was what those around him thought that they knew. Even so, no one we'd talked to had had any idea at all that they would benefit from Mike's death. No one had suspected that anything would be coming to them.

"It was something that he'd mentioned to me several times, but I'd known him for the last five and a half years. I don't know if he ever told anybody else or not."

Okay, so someone killing him for his money was still on the table, although slightly downgraded as a possible motive. For a person to kill Mike in order to inherit from him, that person would need to have reason to believe that they were in Mike's will and that they would be getting some money from him. Given that Mike had been vocal with Emily about leaving his money to charity for the sake of not giving anyone the chance to benefit from his death, it was likely that he never said anything to anyone that would lead them to think that they would be inheriting from him.

"Can you think of anyone who might have been willing to hurt Mike?" Zoey asked.

"Well, gee, I don't think you'd have to look much further than his renters. I know that things weren't always good between him and them. He'd sometimes let things slip when talking to me. He'd make jokes about how dumb someone was not to have their lawyer look over their contract or something else like that."

Mike's renters were already high on our list of suspects. We needed to know if there was anyone else. "Can you think of any others who might have wanted to hurt Mike?"

"Mmmm, his neighbor, Tina, was pretty weird. I don't know if she'd actually get physical with someone, but she wasn't right. I met her a few times, and she gave me the creeps."

"In what way?" I asked.

"It'd be like she'd leave but I felt like she was still there watching us. I don't know. She was just weird. Like someone who might do anything, even though she never did anything. She always just seemed two blinks away from boiling your pet rabbit in your kitchen."

"But you never saw her do anything?"

"No, I didn't. That was just the feeling

I got from her. But you really should be asking Mike's girlfriend about this stuff, not me."

Ohhhh… hello. "He had a girlfriend?" I asked.

Emily shrugged her shoulders. "I'm sure he did. He always did. Mind you, he never kept a girlfriend for long—which I think he preferred it that way. He didn't want anyone getting any ideas that he owed them anything. So, his relationships tended to be short, but… there was always someone."

"But you don't know who?"

"No. He'd mention names sometimes, but I never asked. And it was always a different woman's name."

A car pulled up and parked outside her store. We were almost out of time.

"Emily, can you tell us where you were the day Mike died?"

Emily went back to the checkout counter and retrieved her cell phone. She scrolled through it as she walked back over to us. Finally, she handed it over. There was a picture of her at a podium on a stage. "I was giving a speech at an out-of-state conference for women entrepreneurs. The conference ran for three days —Friday, Saturday, and Sunday—and I was there the whole time. The day that Mike died, I was on a flight home."

She scrolled through the phone some more and showed us a digital airplane ticket. It was marked for ten-thirty AM in Michigan. There was no way she would have been able to make it back in time to kill Mike that morning.

CHAPTER 15

Zoey ran me by the grocery store before we headed back to the café so that I could pick up ingredients for a dinner dish. I wanted to try my hand at making steak hoagies. It would give me a chance to practice making steaks. If I undercooked one of the steaks, I'd know when I cut into it, and I could simply cook it longer. And if I overcooked it, the sandwich would have so many other things going on that hopefully no one would notice how tough the meat was. It was a win-win for all. At least that was how I was choosing to think about it.

"Catch you later," Zoey said, carrying

in the last of the grocery bags through the café's back door into the kitchen.

"Thanks!"

I stuck my head out of the kitchen and gave Melanie a wave to let her know that I was back. The temperature inside felt good. It was clear that Melanie had cycled the heater on and off, making the café cozy without being hot. As always, Melanie had done a great job keeping things going while I was out.

I got to work unpacking grocery bags, and Melanie showed up a couple of minutes later.

"How's everything gone?" I asked.

"Great! Everybody's loving the lasagna."

"Still have enough lasagna left to last another hour and a quarter?"

"I think so."

"Great. After that we'll offer a choice for dinner of lasagna or a steak hoagie."

"Steak hoagie? Yum!"

I sure hoped it would be. I still had to figure out how to make it!

Melanie headed back out to the café floor, and I switched my focus to figuring out how to make a good steak hoagie. I had scanned through a bunch of recipes before going to the grocery store, and now I looked through at least twenty more.

I picked the one with ingredients closest to what I had available and within my skill range and got to work. I was halfway through grilling the third steak when I heard Melanie nervously clear her throat in the kitchen entryway.

"Kylie, you've got some visitors," she said.

Not my husband. Anybody but Dan.

Still holding the two-pronged six-inch fork that I'd been using to flip the steaks, I headed to the kitchen doorway and peeked out.

"Oh!" Standing on the inside of the café door were Winnie, Manny, Patty, and Derek. They were the group of homeless people who had been living in the park next to Mike's house. I'd invited them to come to the café when the weather was due to drop too cold. I guessed that tonight was the night.

The group was huddled close together just inside the café door. They weren't stepping any further inside, and they looked as if they weren't sure they should.

I tossed the sharp pronged fork onto the nearest counter and headed out to greet them. "Come in, come in!" I encouraged with a welcoming smile. "I'm so glad that you could make it."

Out of the corner of my vision, I saw a couple of my other customers eyeing the new group warily. The customers didn't look pleased.

I glanced back at the Cozy Corner and saw that it was empty. There was enough spare space back there for them to store their belongings in a corner. They hadn't brought much. In addition to the space, the fire would be nice for helping them warm up.

"You guys follow me, and I'll get you settled."

"You sure this is okay?" Derek asked as

the group stepped in line behind me. "We don't want to intrude."

"I told you all to come, and you came. I'm thankful you guys came in out of the cold." I meant it, but my customers didn't seem to share the sentiment. The wary looks they gave the group turned to disapproving glares as the four passed by. A moment later, I had two different orders changed to carryouts and a third person simply got up and walked out without canceling their order or requesting it to go.

Seeing the loss of business hurt my checkbook. The café—and I—needed the money. The café needed to start operating in the black and it needed to start doing it soon. But despite that, it was all I could do not to tell those customers not to let the door hit them in their derrières on their way out. Good riddance! I really didn't know what they were getting so upset about. Okay, so I was pretty sure that Derek was high out of his gourd. Manny was slurring his words and swaying a little bit. Patty's large, round eyes were staring at her surroundings like she was sure gremlins were about to jump out at her, and she kept a tight hold of Winnie's hand. As for Winnie, she was doing pretty good—albeit she and more than one of the others could do with a shower and some freshly washed clothes. Baby steps. I wasn't prepared to open my apartment for the use of people I didn't know. The café was a public space, and at least for tonight, the group was welcome to stay all night long.

I left Melanie to take their drink orders and ignored my inner voice that fretted over the combined loss of business plus the expense of hosting non-paying customers. Regardless, I did my best to make delicious steak hoagies. I put as much care and effort into the process as if I was serving the meals to a local food critic, and I got smiles all around when I served them to Mike's previous neighbors.

After that, I sent Melanie on her way, showed the group how to work the jet-engine heater, and made them a platter of snacks so that they'd have something to munch on through the night, and I found some cold medicine for Patty. She was doing much better than when I last saw her, but even so, I wanted her to have it.

If I'd had blankets to give them, I would have, but I didn't really have a blanket for myself. Some nights I used my coat as a blanket. I worked with whatever I had, which wasn't much. So unfortunately, that meant that other than food, warmth, and the cozy corner's comfy furniture, the group was on their own in terms of creature comforts.

Two hours went by with no new customers.

"I'm calling it a night," I told my guests. "Do you need anything before I head upstairs?"

Manny had a chair pulled up right in front of the fireplace. His sleep looked so deep that I worried he was dead, but a snore reassured me otherwise. Derek was on his feet with his long, skeletal arms hugging himself as he gently swayed from side to side. And Patty and Winnie sat in the love seat, Patty's head resting on Winnie's shoulder, asleep.

"We're good," Winnie said with a soft voice, the type used when you didn't want to wake others. "Thank you for this."

I smiled and waved as a silent "you're welcome" before collecting Sage and heading upstairs to my apartment. There, I took a long, hot bath that took me an hour to prep. I ate a steak hoagie that I'd made two hours and forty-five minutes earlier and realized that I should have eaten it sooner to get the full effect of it being served fresh. And then I curled up on my kitchen mattress between the oil-filled heater Zoey had loaned me and my turned on oven. Sage finished off my cocoon of warmth by curling up to sleep snug against the top of my head.

It was a good night, but morning—for me—came too fast. The sky outside was still dark, but I needed to get my day started to take care of the café. Lying on the mattress, I looked around me. Then I patted the top of my head, found Sage, and snuggled her into my arms against my chest.

"No smoke. No fire alarms." Did the building have a fire alarm system? I needed to find out. "And no fire engine sirens." It was a good sign. The café was still intact, at least structurally. My guests hadn't burned it down, yet I knew that there was no telling what I'd find when I went downstairs.

I knew that it was something I should have considered sooner, but I wondered whether or not they would be able to sell any of the heavy duty, industrial kitchen equipment. I had no idea what it would sell for, but I was sure that it was more money than any one of them—or me—had.

"Come on, little girl," I said to Sage. "Let's get going."

I got dressed, splashed freezing cold water on my face—because it was the only temperature available—and headed downstairs. When I reached the bottom of the stairs, I paused with my hand on the doorknob of the door that would lead into the café's kitchen. With the turn of my wrist, my faith in humanity would either be upheld or destroyed.

I was more than a little nervous to find out which.

I opened the door, took a deep breath, and stopped. I took another deep breath. Then another.

Something smelled amazing! Some sort of cookie, I was sure.

"Hello?" I called out. I headed into the kitchen. Everything was still there. And if my practiced eye didn't know better, the kitchen was even cleaner than how I'd left it the night before.

Following my nose, I found the source of heavenly goodness that was making my olfactory senses happy to be alive and my stomach eager to eat. Just outside the kitchen, on the grill's customer counter, was a large platter artfully stacked with three different kinds of cookies. And these weren't store bought cookies like what I usually offered customers. No, these were home-made... or rather café made. There were chocolate chip, oatmeal raisin, and peanut butter.

I picked up a chocolate chip cookie. It was still warm to the touch. I took a bite, and my eyes rolled back in my head. It was the best cookie I'd eaten in my life. Needing to make sure that the quality of the other types of cookies were just as good (or so I told myself), I had a peanut butter and an oatmeal one as well. If anything, they were even better than the chocolate chip cookie.

Next to the platter was a note. The handwriting was terrible, but I was able to make out what the note said: "More batter in fridge. Made lots. Freeze some."

Taking the note with me, I went to the walk-in cooler. Sure enough, as promised, I found three large bowls filled almost to the brim with the cookie dough batter. It was enough for me to make cookies throughout the day and still have cookie dough to freeze this evening. I'd be able to have the café smelling of cookies all day long and then some.

And that's just what I did.

CHAPTER 16

"Stir it a little more," Brenda said.

"Like this?" I asked.

"Right, like that. Good. Give the bottom of the pan a good scraping to get up the good bits."

I did as Brenda instructed. She was helping me make a bacon and potato hash to serve with the frittata Lorraine she'd already helped me make. And we'd prepped several casserole dishes worth of spinach and ricotta stuffed shells with tomato sauce. I'd be able to pop them in the oven this evening for the dinner customers, and any leftover trays could be wrapped and put in the freezer for another day.

"What's that smell?" called out a familiar voice. It was Brad.

"Do you smell something?" I asked Brenda, instantly worried. Of course there was the obvious. The dish we were making had bacon, potatoes, onions and bell peppers. But with a question like, "What's that smell?" I worried that something out in the café had gone terribly wrong. Winnie, Manny, Derek and Patty had stayed all night in the café, and it was true that they had been a bit behind in their hygiene, but I hadn't noticed anything off smelling when I'd checked the café's dining area that morning. But Brad had a cop's nose. Maybe he'd been specially trained to suss out scents that were going unnoticed by me. Maybe there was a dead rat that had gotten lodged somewhere in the walls. Maybe some of the electrical wires had gotten frayed and the air was filling with a burnt electrical smell.

Leaving Brenda to oversee the hash, I

hurried out to the café. "What's wrong? What do you smell?" There was no keeping the worry from my voice.

"Only a little piece of heaven," Brad said. "These little babies right here." He pressed his palms against the edge of the grill's serving counter and leaned in close to the large, dome-covered platter that was stacked with cookies. Closing his eyes, he breathed in deep.

"Oh!" I laughed. "You had me worried."

"The only thing to worry about is what you'll feed your other customers when I walk out of here with the whole dish." He managed to pull his attention away from the cookies and look at me. "Did you make these?" There was a disbelieving note in his voice.

I tried not to take offense to his incredulous tone. I could have made the cookies—if I'd had the recipe, maybe some help, half a day, and enough ingredients to work through five or six trial runs.

Trying to bluff, I crossed arms and

asked, "What do you think?" The intention had been to shame him into conceding that I could have made the cookies, but his lopsided grin and knowing smile told me that my attempt at subterfuge wasn't working.

"I think somebody took pity on you and brought these in." Well, he was partially right. "What are you going to do when somebody wants to special order a bunch of them but you don't know how to make them?"

His level of presumption was reaching arrogant levels. "Sometimes I really hate you," I said.

Instead of getting upset at that, Brad just laughed. "Breakfast ready?"

I nodded.

"I'll make coffee while you get me a plate."

Five minutes later, Brad had gotten two pots of coffee brewed and was two bites into his breakfast. "Oh my gosh. How much are you charging for this?"

I told him.

"Add a dollar. This is excellent."

I nearly tripped over my own feet. "Come again?"

Brad's smile was as cocky as ever. "Don't get too full of yourself, Berry."

"No, no… I heard you. You said 'excellent.' You called something I cooked 'excellent.'"

Brad narrowed his eyes, then called out, "How you doin' this morning, Brenda?" The woman hadn't made a peep and hadn't shown her face. There was no way for him to have known that she was there. Except, that is, for the excellence of my food.

"Doin' good!" Brenda called back, and Brad's grin went from cocky to downright smug.

"You know that price I quoted you?"

"Yeah?"

"You can add two dollars to it." And with that, I abandoned him to eat his breakfast alone.

Mid-morning, Brenda left and my waiter Sam made his way in. Together we tackled the lunch crowd, and it was close to qualifying as an actual crowd. I kept making small batches of fresh cookies all throughout the morning and into the afternoon. I'd see their effect as people walked by the front of the café. They'd be going past, focused on their day, then their fast, purposeful gait would falter only to leave them stopping and staring. At least half of those people took the extra steps of walking through the door. One woman even ordered two dozen cookies to go. They were a huge hit and really did a lot to bring in new customers throughout the day, not to mention extra money.

As for lunch itself, I made more of the same steak hoagies that I'd made last night. At the start of serving lunch, I listed them on the Oops board at a hefty discount. By the end of the lunch service, I'd erased them off the Oops board and was charging a price that had the café operating in the black—at least for those hours.

We stayed so busy that poor Sam didn't even have a chance to crack open a single textbook and get in some extra studying. But he didn't seem to mind. I'd gotten a glance at some of the tips that were being left behind, and he was doing well. I was happy to see it.

The lunch rush slowed to a trickle around two, and the café only had three customers in it when Zoey showed up at three. She took one look around at how empty the café was, stole an oatmeal and raisin cookie, and said, "Let's go. Sam's got this. I wanna talk to Clara."

"Why Clara?" She was one of Mike's renters. She had a little hole in the wall coffee shop right next to Susie's hair salon. In fact, she called it, *Little Java Hole.*

"With her shop right next to Susie's, she might be able to drop some piece of information that either pins it on Susie or clears her name."

That made sense, but for some reason I wasn't eager to go talk to Clara.

My hesitation had me doing a quick self-check as to why, and I realized that if Susie was guilty that I didn't want to know. Not *really* know. Not know without a shadow of a doubt.

"Maybe we could go hit up the County Clerk's Office and learn more about the properties Mike owned," I offered as a counter option.

Zoey pointed at herself. "Severe allergy. To all places suffering a bureaucratic infestation."

I was going to take that as a no.

Clara's it was. After that, I wanted to track down whoever it was that made these cookies!

CHAPTER 17

Zoey parked the car in front of Clara's coffee shop, *Little Java Hole*, and I felt instantly guilty. Right next door to the coffee shop was Susie's hair salon, *Susie's Clip & Dye*. But we weren't going in there. No, we were headed into the coffee shop to talk to Clara about Susie, to see if Clara had any dirt to sling in Susie's direction. It made me feel like one of the mean girls, like I was going behind a friend's back to trash talk her.

"This place has the best coffee," Zoey said as we got out of the car.

A squeak of jealous complaint escaped me, but other than that, I managed to hold my feelings in. Where they could fester and rot.

Screw it.

"What do you mean she's got the best coffee?" I had been busting my butt to do everything I knew to do to become known as a place where people could get great coffee. After all, Clara's little coffee shop was right next door to Susie's shop, but she had promoted my café to her customers and had even gone out of her way to buy coffee from me.

Zoey didn't bother to placate me. Instead she merely shrugged and smiled. No apology in her expression whatsoever.

We headed into Clara's shop. The second the door opened and I stepped inside, I was enveloped in an aroma I could only describe as warm vanilla drinking espresso in Italy. I know it didn't make sense, but that was how her shop made me feel. The inner atmosphere of the shop was dim, and there was an eclectic collection of comfortable chairs placed throughout her shop with a variety of small, unobtrusive tables. Every chair had at least one small surface available within arm's reach on which to put their drink.

Her clientele had a slightly preppy college look with some professionals tucked into the mix. Of the twenty-five possible seats, over half of them were full. I counted four wait staff. Four. On a late Saturday afternoon. My café was at least triple the size of her small, intimate space, yet I could only afford one wait staff at a time. Even then, I was usually operating in the red.

I glanced at her prices and squeaked again. A simple cup of coffee cost almost four times what I charged. And she had lots of customers. It wasn't fair.

"Can I help you?" a slender woman of indeterminate age in a cream-colored peasant blouse asked from behind the serving counter. She was slowly turning a crank handle on top of a small wooden box, and her effortless beauty and high cheekbones made me think of Michelle Pfeiffer.

"Hi, Clara," Zoey said, and we made our way over to the counter. "What flavor are you grinding?" she asked, and it was then that I realized what the small box was. It was a manual coffee grinder.

"The house special of the day. A luscious hazelnut dark roast. Would you like a cup? I'll have the grind done in another twenty minutes."

Twenty minutes! I wanted to hit my head against the wall. I used a mechanical grinder for mine. It took it twenty seconds, and I'd thought that that was too long. How did she stay in business? Why were people willing to pay so much for her coffee?

"Do you have any of that Mexican spiced hot chocolate in?"

"I sure do. Want a cup?"

"Make it two," she said. "Then if you don't mind sitting with us for a few minutes, we'd like to ask you some questions.

Clara made a surprised "oh" face but recovered quickly. "You two grab a seat. I'll bring your drinks and we'll sit and talk." She had a confidante's voice, the type of person you felt safe telling your deepest, darkest secrets to.

I followed Zoey to a corner nook that didn't have anyone sitting immediately nearby. I sat in a chair that was so big and so comfortable that I could have curled up and gone to sleep in it. Zoey sat in a wing backed chair that looked less sleep-inducing but had a grandiose quality that still looking very comfortable.

Clara joined us about five minutes later with delicate china coffee cups in hand. She passed one to each of us.

I sniffed at the dark, rich brew inside the cup and was surprised. The aroma was complex with layered notes. Chocolate. Chilies. Cinnamon. And those were only the notes that I could name.

I took a sip and moaned, sinking deeper into my chair. The spiced Mexican hot chocolate was very, very good. I hated to think of how much it cost and was glad that Zoey was treating.

"What can I help you ladies with?" Clara asked, ready to get to business. I could respect that. She was running her shop and it was the middle of the day. She had better things to do than to sit with us.

"Did you kill Mike?" Zoey asked.

Clara's head jerked back as if slapped, but then she broke out in laughter and covered her heart with her hand. The laughter went on for so long that she was having to wipe tears from the corners of her eyes by the time she stopped.

"That man was a terrible man," Clara said. "I don't blame Susie for what she did. Not one little bit."

"What did Susie do?" I asked.

"Well, kill Mike, of course!"

Zoey and I looked at each other. Then I asked Clara, "Did you see Susie kill Mike?"

"Well, I'm still alive, aren't I?" she answered with the flip of her hand. I didn't understand her response and stayed quiet, hoping for more. Finally, looking a little annoyed for having to spell it out, she said, "If I'd seen Susie kill Mike, well I'd already be dead, wouldn't I?"

"So you're saying that Susie killed Mike," I said, "and that if Susie thought you had any evidence against her that she'd kill you, too."

"That is the way these things work, isn't it? You murder someone and then tie up all the loose ends? *I* am not a loose end."

"But you know that Susie did it, that she killed Mike," I pressed.

"Yes."

"How do you know it?"

Clara looked at me like I was dumb. "Well who else could have done it? Susie was at his house that very morning. And I saw her come back. I said it right then when I saw her, too. I said to myself, that girl's out for blood. And I. Was. Right."

"What time was it when you saw Susie?" Zoey asked.

"Just before eleven."

According to what we'd previously learned from Susie, that would have been before Mike had died. It would have been after she'd gone to see him the first of two times that morning.

"And how did Susie look? Zoey asked.

"I've already told you. She was mad. She had steam rolling right out of her ears." Clara pantomimed the description by rolling her hands next to her ears.

"How were her clothes and her hair?" I asked. If Susie had gotten into a physical fight with Mike, it was likely that her clothes and hair might have been disheveled afterward.

"Her clothes and hair? The woman is a professional stylist. Her hair was the same it ever was. Perfect. I didn't notice anything about her clothes. Couldn't even tell you what she'd been wearing."

"Did you see Susie leave a little later that day, at about noon?"

"Nooo, no. I left and went home shortly after I saw her walk by my shop all mad."

"You went home?" I asked, surprised.

"Had a splitting headache. It felt like someone was taking an ice pick and jabbing it through my temple to right behind my eyes. Terrible. I had to go."

"Did you go alone?"

"Well, of course. I couldn't burden any of my employees with my personal problems. I needed them here to run the shop."

"Was there anyone at home?"

"Not a soul. Just quiet solitude. Exactly what my headache needed."

"So," I said, "after you saw Susie come back mad, you left. But nobody went with you, and nobody saw you at home."

"That's what I said."

A light went on in my head. Clara didn't have an alibi.

"Had you known who Susie was going to see that morning?" Zoey asked.

"Oh, yeah. She'd been over here half the morning before that, fussing and fuming about Mike, about what a lowlife he was and how he was killing her."

"Killing her?" If that had really been how Susie had felt—that Mike had been killing her—then she might have felt like she was acting in self-defense by killing Mike. "She used that word?"

"Ohhhh, she used that word plus a whole lot more!" Clara laughed. "Why I'd never seen the woman so mad." She laughed some more. "Better warn Betty. Susie might be coming after her next."

My head was spinning with the information that was coming out of Clara's mouth.

"Betty?" I asked.

"Yes?" Clara responded. Her expression was completely innocent, but I was starting to feel like it was all a guise. A foul ruse. Suddenly her hot cocoa wasn't tasting quite as good.

When Clara didn't offer up any clarification about Betty from my gentle prompting, I tried again. I was sure that Clara was playing dumb about what I'd been asking just to be annoying.

"What does Betty need to be warned about?" I asked.

"Well, that she'll be next!" Clara answered, again looking at me like I was a simpleton. As for me, I wanted to simultaneously hit my head against the wall and retrieve a pair of pliers so that I could yank Clara's teeth from her head, one by one. That's what it felt like I was needing to do to get the information I needed out of her.

"*Why* would Betty be next?" I asked, doing my best to keep my voice casual and easygoing. I only marginally succeeded, and I saw Clara's eyes narrow venomously in response.

"Susie hates Betty."

"Why?" Where were those pliers?

"Well, Betty runs a beauty parlor just like Susie, and Susie's convinced that Betty is stealing her clients. Offering them discounts. Telling them made-up stories about Susie botching jobs and people losing their hair."

"Does Betty do those things?" I asked.

"Oh, yeah. Definitely. Betty would do anything to make Susie look bad. Hates her."

"So not only does Susie hate Betty, but Betty hates Susie, too?"

"You're on the money now," Clara answered, answering slowly with no small amount of patronization in her voice.

I leaned to the side and looked out the

glass front of Clara's shop. Even from where I sat, I could see Betty's storefront across the street. If I could see it from where I was sitting, that meant that Betty could definitely see Susie when Susie came back mad from having talked to Mike.

Clara excused herself and returned to running her disgustingly successful coffee shop, while Zoey and I finished our cups of cocoa and mulled over what we'd learned. When we'd walked into Clara's shop that morning, we'd had one strong possible culprit in mind: Susie. Now, leaving, we had three.

Susie, Clara and Betty.

CHAPTER 18

I stopped on the way out to Zoey's car.

"What's up?" she asked.

"Don't you think we should stop in and check on Susie?" I felt guilty coming over to her stomping grounds to dig up dirt about her without even checking in to see how she was doing. Before all of this had happened, I had considered her a friend—a very recent addition to a very limited number of people, but still a friend.

"We could," Zoey said, and we detoured the fifteen feet necessary to take us to *Susie's Clip & Dye's* front door.

Inside the shop, easy listening music played but there wasn't any light-hearted banter to accompany it, as was often the case when a beautician had a client in the chair. Instead, there was only Susie sitting in her chair, with her legs crossed and an open magazine on her lap. Her eyes were puffy like she'd been crying, but not recently.

There was no smell of hairspray or any other chemicals common to such a shop, and the place looked immaculate.

"Hi, you two!" Susie said, getting up from her chair. Her smile was huge and her face was bright with happiness. She got up from the chair, put the magazine aside, and gave us both warm hugs. I hugged Susie back, but I saw Zoey go stiff. Exuberant expressions of affection weren't really her thing. "Who's first?" Susie asked, stepping away and giving her chair a pat.

"Oh, no, it's nothing like that," I said, and Susie's expression instantly fell. Her lit face literally dimmed, as if a dreary winter storm cloud had passed overhead.

Not wanting her to feel snubbed, I quickly continued. "We just came from next door, Clara's *Little Java Hole*." I had not imagined that Susie's face could grow any more downtrodden, but it did. There was a hint of dourness as well as her eyes cut to the side to glare through the wall at Clara's shop.

Susie plopped back down into her chair, crossed her legs, and flipped her magazine open once more on her lap. "And what did the queen of coffee have to say?"

Definitely no love lost between them, I mused. "She told us that you killed Mike."

Surprise was completely absent from Susie's face, but annoyance was in abundance. She rolled her eyes and then flipped through her magazine.

"You're not surprised?" I gently probed. I needed to understand what was going on here.

"Nooo," Susie said, sounding like a petulant fourteen-year-old girl.

It was Zoey's turn. "She said you'd kill Betty next."

"That witch!" Susie slammed her magazine shut. "She tries to make like she's all sweet and nice, but she's a slithering snake, wiggling around on her belly in the grass." She did a curvy wave with her arm to demonstrate. "I once saw her put a laxative in a woman's coffee, but first she put an out of order sign on her bathroom and locked the doors."

"Wow." That really was a mean thing to do. I couldn't imagine ever doing that to a customer of mine.

"Yeah… Then, when the lady and her husband went running out of the shop in search for a bathroom, Clara called the cops on them for not paying their bill."

"She didn't!" I was aghast.

"She did! And, when Terrance at the *Saucy Dog* hired one of her waitresses away, Clara went in there in the middle of the lunch crowd and claimed that she'd gotten food poisoning from his food. Said she'd been in the hospital for a week from it and was going to sue him if he didn't pay the medical bill."

"Um, did she get food poisoning from him?" I knew it was silly to ask, but I didn't know what had happened and needed to be sure. I wanted to know just how vile and devious a person Clara was.

"No, she didn't get food poisoning from him. I don't think she'd ever eaten there in her life. But she didn't care. She ruined his business for that day and then told him that if he ever stole another one of her waitresses again, she'd make sure the place went out of business."

"So, Clara's kind of big on revenge." I shot Zoey a look. It didn't go unnoticed by Susie. She gasped.

"Yes! Yes, that's right! She does like revenge! Maybe she killed him!"

Zoey cracked her knuckles. "Know of anything she had against him?"

Susie's eyes got big and round, and she started wagging her finger at the adjoining wall between her shop and Clara's. "Yes, I do. Her body."

"What?" I couldn't believe my ears.

Had we stumbled onto figuring out who Mike had been seeing when he died?

"I think that they had an affair."

"Oh…" Susie's "I think" kind of ruined the moment for me. "But you don't *know*?"

"Well, no… But, I've heard rumors. And I've been over there when Mr. Pratt was there. She'd coo at him."

"Coo at him?"

"Yeah, she'd make like he was some sweet little boy or something. She'd pinch his cheeks and talk all sweet to him. She'd stand up close to him, loop her arm through his, and press herself against him. I saw him blush once!"

"Wow…" That information certainly did put a new spin on things. "Has she ever bragged about having an affair with him or did you ever hear about them going out together?"

"Nooo," Susie said, losing some of her enthusiasm for her argument.

That's when a thought occurred to me. Clara was a beautiful woman. She had an elegant charm about her that I wasn't sure she could turn off if she wanted to. I imagined that if she was standing alone in a corner at some party, the party would eventually congregate to her. She had a vivacious magnetism.

As for Susie, she was no slouch. She'd been head cheerleader and the "it" girl in high school. Even now in her late thirties, she would have been able to hold her head up with pride even when wearing a string bikini while standing next to a high school gymnast. She was gorgeous.

"Do you know if Clara ever had any contract issues with her rent?"

Susie's face scrunched up in thought. "When I started to get concerned about my situation, I tried to ask Clara about her contract, but I didn't want to be too obvious about it. I don't trust Clara. She makes me think that if she had something to use against me, something that made me vulnerable, that she would. So, I didn't want her to know what Mr. Pratt was doing to me by drastically increasing my rent. But I talked to her, tried to feel her out. Asked her if Mr. Pratt had ever acted like a bully to her."

"What'd she say?" I asked.

"She just laughed, said that Mr. Pratt —she called him Mike—was a big pushover and that you just had to know how to handle him." She shook her head. "I walked away from that conversation with the impression that he hadn't jacked her rent up, and I know that her business is doing well. I mean, that's what he did to me. My business started doing well—had been doing well—and he increased my rent by almost three hundred percent."

I latched on to what she'd said about how her business was doing. I'd guessed that she hadn't had much business when Zoey and I walked in, but I wanted to hear it from her. "Things aren't going well now?" I asked.

Susie shook her head. Scowling, she said, "No." Then her eyes cut to her front windows to stare across the street. "Betty's telling everyone not to trust me. It's nothing new, not exactly, but since Mr. Pratt... well, it's gotten worse."

"How so?" Zoey asked.

"Used to be she told people that I'd burn up their hair and make it brittle from my perms. Told people I'd botch the color job. I'd heard she was even telling people that I'd given people bald spots." She looked at me. "That's why I did that ad campaign using real customers. I'd wanted people to see what I could do and to know that they could trust me. I figured that my work would speak louder than Betty's lies."

It had only been a couple of weeks since I'd sat in Susie's salon chair for a free cut and highlight in exchange for her taking before and after pictures of me to use on her Facebook page. And she had a twelve-by-nine poster board of the results sitting in her shop window, right next to several other posters. I assumed that the other posters were of other local townsfolk, the same as me.

"And your business was growing before... but now it's not?" I asked.

"It's gone dead," Susie said and then

grimaced, presumably at her choice of words.

"So what's changed?"

"Mr. Pratt's dead and Betty's telling everyone I did it, at least I think that's what's happening. Clara jumping on that bandwagon sure doesn't help. She really told you that I killed him?"

"With absolute certainty," Zoey answered.

Behind us, Susie's shop door opened.

"Come on in!" Susie said with an eager excitement. "I've just had a time slot open up and I can take care of you right now."

I turned around to see a mother with her pre-teen daughter. The daughter had curly red hair that had yet to be tamed. I felt her pain, given my own red locks. My hair wasn't nearly as curly as the little girl's, but it had still taken me years to figure out how to make it look its best.

Zoey and I made a quiet exit and left Susie to fawn over her new customers.

Back in the car, Zoey asked, "You need to get back for the dinner rush?"

"I do, but let's go by Mike's place first."

"We breaking in? I want to wait until nightfall if we're breaking in."

"Nooo, no. This is something much more important than Mike's place. I want to swing by the park next door to Mike's. I want to know who made those cookies!"

CHAPTER 19

Finding my homeless sleepover crew was a bust. By the time I got back to the café, I'd been to three different parks, two homeless shelters, five churches, and had been yelled at by a man because I hadn't wanted to buy his used sneakers, covered in what I really, really hoped was paint. But walking back into the café reminded me that the effort had been worth it even if it hadn't panned out. The place smelled of vanilla, peanut butter, and sugar, and I stopped and stared at all the customers I had. I was sure that the turnout was because of the cookies. There were as many people in my café as there had been at Clara's coffee shop. Of course, my café was way, way bigger, but still. I had more customers than her!

My head filled with a sing-song nanny-nanny-boo-boo, and I had to remind myself that I was no longer five years old. But having so many customers was amazing to see. There were a whole sixteen of them! Yet the sight instantly filled me with guilt. I was the chef, and I'd been gone for well over two and a half hours.

Melanie was rushing by, and I quickly beckoned her over. "What's everyone been eating?" I asked.

"The cookies. They're loving them! I've been baking small batches ever since I got in, and they've been selling just as fast as I bake them."

I had to find out who made them!

"Great job!" I told Melanie. "You keep doing what you've been doing, and I'll get some food started."

I rushed into the kitchen. I grabbed one of the casserole trays of stuffed pasta shells, took off the cellophane, and popped it into the oven. Then, after checking my notes that Brenda had given me about how to fix them, I took the tray back out and pre-heated the oven. *Then* I put in the tray!

It was going to be a while, though. I had sixteen paying customers in my café —and it wasn't even lunch! In fact, it wasn't even quite full-fledged dinner. It was more pre-dinner. Yet they were here, drinking my coffee… and eating somebody else's cookies.

If I ran out of that cookie dough, people were going to ask for more cookies and I wasn't going to have any for them. It was a thought that made my heart race in my chest. I had to find out how to make those cookies! My life as I knew it would end and the café would go under if I didn't!

"Plan B," I said and forced myself to take a deep, calming breath. "Buy more cookies from the store." Who was I kidding? My customers would revolt. They'd carry pitchforks and light torches. I'd be run out of town!

Disgraced. All because of a freaking cookie.

I was starting to hate those cookies.

Pushing all cookie thoughts out of my head, I waved Melanie over to the kitchen.

"Let all of the customers know that an entree of steak salad is now available at an Oops Board discount and that stuffed shells will be available in an hour, at full price."

She nodded and was off, and I added the steak salad to the Oops board and the stuffed shells to the regular menu board. This was a rare night indeed. Tonight's customers would actually have a choice between entrees.

Back in the kitchen, I was a flurry of activity and was able to fill six orders for steak salad a half an hour later.

Outside in the café, I heard the sound of a jet taking off. It was the forced air heater. Somebody was messing with it and it didn't need to be messed with. Out front, the temperature was cool but comfortable, and back in the kitchen, I was having to wipe perspiration off my forehead.

I hurried out the kitchen door to chase off whatever hooligan thought it was time to have some fun but stopped in my tracks. Joel was squatting next to the contraption, playing with it, but as soon as he saw me, he turned it off.

"Hi!" I said, heading over to him. "Thank you so much for arranging this."

"It's done okay for you?"

"It's done great. Amazing, actually. I'm pretty sure that this place would be empty right now without this thing." Even with the siren call of magic cookies. "Is your friend needing it back yet?"

"No, he said keep it as long as you need. Hey, while I've got you with, um, nobody else around"—I was sure he was referring to Brad—"I wanted to ask you about that date we never got to have. How 'bout you let me take you out Tuesday night?"

I opened my mouth to say yes, but Susie's image flashed in my mind. I hesitated, and Joel saw the hesitation. His smile faltered.

"Unless you don't want to," he said.

"I want to!" Okay, I said that waaayyyy too eagerly. I made myself pause a beat to regain some composure. "It's just that—"

"You're investigating Mike Pratt's murder, aren't you?" He dipped his chin, and I saw the twinkle in his eye. "You found anything out? Able to give a guy an exclusive news scoop?"

This time I thought of Brad and how furious he'd be if I did find new evidence but then leaked the existence of that evidence to the press instead of giving the information exclusively to him. It was the type of thing that could really mess up his investigation.

I decided to sidestep the question. "About that date, next Sunday night, a week from now?"

Joel did a slow nod of his head. "So… by that timeline, you believe that you will have the murder solved by the end of the week?"

I opened my mouth and squeaked

before I managed to regain control of my voice. "That's not what I said."

Joel's smile grew big. "Sure it is. It's just not the words you used."

That sneaky ba—

"Hey, Joel!" a man's voice called as he walked in the café's front door along with what looked like ten other people. "We're here."

"Hey!" Joel waved. "I'll be right there." He turned back to me. "Employee monthly meeting. Decided to have it here tonight. Bring in some extra business for you."

I leaned to the side to see past Joel in order to do a head count. Twelve people! With Joel, that would make thirteen. On one hand, the café was set to turn the biggest profit it had ever made since I'd taken over. On the other hand, Joel had sprung on me the task of serving dinner to thirteen customers all at once! I could handle thirteen customers... if each came in half an hour apart, maybe!

What had the man done to me?

Whatever he'd done, he didn't seem to

notice. I got a shoulder squeeze from him and then off he went to join his colleagues.

I didn't know if I should laugh or cry, but neither one would feed these people. On top of that, we hadn't finalized our date plans. Were we on or not?

I hurried into the kitchen and got to work prepping the ingredients for the steak salad, a simple tossed salad to go with the pasta shells, and I called Melanie into the kitchen to cook up a fresh batch of cookies. When Melanie got done, she left but then stuck her head back in.

"You've got a customer at the grill's bar. It's one of your regulars. Want me to get them?"

My mind raced through the possible list. Joel was already here. Zoey was doing Zoey stuff. Brad was more of a morning guy. That left Angela and Jack.

"No, I've got them. Thanks, Melanie." I headed out to the grill and there found a stoic-as-ever Jack. Behind him, the café was teeming with life, and there was a soft murmur of voices that I was unused to hearing. The place was usually so quiet.

"Hi, Jack!" I said, abandoning the kitchen. The various ingredients were prepped, and all that was left was to assemble the entrees as the orders came in.

"Hi yourself," Jack said. He glanced behind himself and then turned back around to look at me. "I see you're well."

"In more ways than one." I could feel myself beaming like a proud mama. My baby—the café—was doing great.

"Congratulations," he said.

"Thank you," I said, glancing around us. Nobody else was around. This was my chance. I could be bold. I could finally ask the question that had been burning a hole in my mind every time I'd seen Jack.

"Jack, I've got a question. Two questions, actually."

"Yes?"

"Would you be able to tell me what properties Mike Pratt owned?"

"No."

"It's confidential?"

"Yes, but that's not why I can't tell you. I'm not involved at that level of detail, so I simply don't know the answer. But in addition to that, that it's confidential information is why I *wouldn't* tell you even if I knew."

I wondered if Zoey could hack the bank's records… then wondered if Jack could read my expression that I was wondering if Zoey could hack the bank's records.

"And your second question?" Jack asked.

"I was considering getting a loan."

"Oh, that's a bad idea."

"It is?"

"Yes, borrowing money at the cost of money is always a bad idea. It's making your money work against you instead of for you. Your money should *make* you money, not *cost* you money."

I couldn't stop my mouth. I couldn't get my foot up there fast enough. "But your bank offers loans?"

"Yes, it does."

"And,"—I was operating purely on a

hunch—"did you get a loan to start your bank?"

"Yes, I did."

"But I shouldn't get a loan?"

"No, you shouldn't."

"Because it's a bad idea..."

"No. Because it is a *terrible* idea."

I was having trouble wrapping my head around this, and decided that my best option was to blindly accept what he was telling me. The richest man I knew was giving me money advice. The least I could do was listen.

"If you need money," Jack continued, "you could get a job."

I glanced around me again, at all of the people in my café, people I was preparing food for.

"A side job," Jack amended. "Something on the side to bring in the extra money you need. I do know some people."

I was scared. Jack knew people, and I wasn't sure if those people were the moguls of industry or the mafia's elite. The man was gravitas incarnate. He could have made Vito Corleone, the Godfather, look away in a staring contest. I could see him rubbing elbows with the kings and queens of nations. Yet these people, whoever they were, were people Jack wanted to introduce me to.

It could be good, or it could be very, very bad.

"So, what do you say?" he asked.

"Yes, definitely yes," I said, not meaning a word of it. But no way was I going to tell the man no.

"Good!" His face lit up in a rare smile. "Now tell me about these cookies."

The damn cookies! I refrained from hitting my forehead on the counter.

"They're wonderful, aren't they?" I said. I was not ready to admit to Jack that I'd had nothing to do with them.

"Who made them?"

That time I did hit my head on the counter.

"Now, now. I'm sure it's not that bad," he consoled.

"I'm not sure who made them," I

confessed. "I've been looking everywhere to find out."

"Good. Executing a plan is good."

"Can I get you anything for dinner? Want some cookies? Coffee?"

"Actually, I need to be able to feed my whole family and the business associates that I am hosting for dinner. The food needs to be excellent, and I want to save my wife the trouble of having to do so much cooking. I'd much rather have her by my side as we entertain our guests. Do you have any suggestions?"

"Oh, wow… Well, there's an amazing Italian place on the other side of town, and I've heard great things about the Greek restaurant near the interstate."

"Kylie."

"Yes?"

"What suggestions do *you* have that I can buy from *you* to feed my family?" he spoke slowly, as if to a very young child.

"Oh! Me!"

"Yes, Kylie. You."

"Right! Okay…" I thought a moment. "Okay, I could send you home with a whole, large casserole of stuffed shells. Pop it in the oven, let it get hot and bubbly, and you're done!"

"And a salad? Can you make a family-style bowl of salad?"

"I can." I said it with so much pride that a person would have thought that I was talking about whether or not I could climb Mt. Everest.

"With some of those wonderful, crisp bacon crumbles on top?"

"Yes," I said, confirming that I could but with sooo much less confidence than a second before. I did my best to hide my uncertainty.

"And the shells, are they any good?"

I started to open my mouth to say that they were, but decided to let him be the judge instead. "I've got a tray due to come out of the oven right now. Let me go get you a sample, and you can decide for yourself." My confidence was returning. I was positive that those shells were amazing!

"That sounds good."

I ran to the kitchen, burned my hands

rushing to get the wonderfully gooey shells out of the oven, and scooped one into a dish for him. I bounced on my toes with barely contained excitement when I put it in front of him. I felt like a little kid trying to impress my dad.

Jack took a bite. He chewed. He paused. He took another bite. "Mmmm, this is good!"

Rockets and fireworks went off behind my eyes.

"I'll take a whole tray, the family-style salad, and three dozen cookies to go."

Yep, this was the café's best night ever!

CHAPTER 20

"I'm not going to hack into Jack's bank," Zoey said under her breath.

It was pretty early in the morning, and I was surprised to see her at the café. She was sporting her oft-worn Cleopatra eyeliner, but this morning it was in a vivid jade.

"I didn't think I'd be seeing you until lunch." Not even Brad had made it in yet.

"Haven't been to sleep. I'll sleep later." She twisted around in her seat and sent a not-so-surreptitious glare at the couple sitting at one of the small tables next to the windows that ran alongside Main Street. But this wasn't any couple. This was Agatha and her new beau, Conrad. "What is she doing with him?"

If Agatha and Conrad hadn't been so goo-goo eyed for each other, I would have been more worried about them being bothered by Zoey's harsh glances. But as it was, they only had eyes for each other. They were holding hands and looking sigh-worthy sweet together. They made an adorable couple—at least that was my opinion. Zoey obviously had other thoughts.

"Why can't she see what a user he is? Why's he even still here? Mike's funeral was days ago. It's time for him to go back to Florida already."

I decided to distract Zoey by bringing her back to the original conversation. "And why can't you hack into Jack's bank?"

Zoey turned her attention to me. "I didn't say I couldn't—I said I wouldn't. I hack into his bank and the FBI will be all over me. Once they get the scent of somebody's stink, you just can't shake 'em."

"Um, you saying this from experience?"

"Maybe."

I wasn't going to ask, but if hacking Jack's bank was out of the question, that had us back to going to the County Clerk's Office and searching through the property deeds. Even then, that wouldn't give us any information as to what types of contracts he had with who.

I went to the kitchen and fixed a plate of biscuits and gravy for Zoey, unasked. I hoped that their potential deliciousness would lull her into feeling only a mild dislike of Conrad instead of the rampant hate that seemed to have swallowed her whole.

As for Agatha and Conrad, they'd requested a quiche Lorraine for two, and there was no way that I'd been able to refuse. So, I'd mustered up every memory and every tip Brenda had given me about how to make a frittata Lorraine and made it in a pie shell instead. I baked it until it stopped jiggling in the middle, and hoped that it was cooked through.

I first served Zoey her plate of biscuits and gravy, and then, with her preoccupied, I took Agatha and Conrad their quiche.

"This looks wonderful, dear," Agatha praised as I set the quiche down between them. They already had plates, utensils and coffee.

I held my breath when Conrad cut into the egg pie, and then let it out when he lifted up the slice and the egg filling proved itself to be solid all the way through.

Agatha noticed and gave me a little wink.

By the time I got back to Zoey, she had half her breakfast plate eaten. "You need to patent this or something. It's amazing. You could serve it to crack addicts to help them forget about crack."

"Really?" It might have been the nicest thing anybody had ever said to me.

"Really. But, you know, I think you might have something with this bank hacking stuff. I could hack into Conrad's bank. I could prove to Agatha once and for all that he's a swindling, no good crook out to use her for whatever he can get."

"You're willing to hack whatever bank Conrad banks with but not Jack's?"

"This is different. We're talking about Aggie here. Protecting her would be worth hacking into Conrad's bank accounts. You can learn a lot about a man from his bank accounts."

I had no doubt that she was right.

The café's front door opened, and Brad walked in.

"I saw that, Jin," he said, calling Zoey by her last name. "I saw that." He made snake eyes back and forth between them with his index and middle fingers.

"Saw what?" Zoey asked as Brad reached the counter and sat down next to her.

"You said the word bank. I saw it."

"You saw it?"

"I saw it. Through the front windows. I read your lips."

"You're a pervert, you know that, right?"

"And you're a criminal," Brad shot back at her.

"Prove it."

"I'm working on it."

"Did you guys get along before I moved to town? Is this new?" I hadn't noticed any animosity between them when I'd arrived. Of course, Zoey had been teary-eyed and overwhelmed with grief when I'd arrived. She hadn't really been in Brad-banter shape, and maybe Brad had taken pity on her and left her alone because of it.

"What are you talking about?" Brad said. "We get along."

"Yeah," Zoey seconded.

I looked between the two of them. They weren't sounding sarcastic. I believed that they believed that they both got along with each other, even though Brad thought that Zoey was a criminal and Zoey thought that Brad was a nosy cop who should mind his own business.

I gave up and didn't press it further. "How come you're late? I had to make the coffee myself."

"Oh..." Brad said, his eyes cutting away to the full coffee pots. He sounded genuinely disappointed.

"Wanna make it again?" I asked.

His expression brightened. "You wouldn't mind?"

"Naw, I can save what I made and use it to make mocha milkshakes later. I've got some ice cream that needs to be used up before it gets ice crystals on it."

I transferred the coffee I'd made to a large pitcher and stored it in the walk-in cooler, and Brad made his magically superior coffee. I'd tried to make it like him a dozen times over, but somehow his was always better. But mine would be just fine mixed in with chocolate syrup and vanilla ice cream.

Zoey had emptied her plate by the time I made it back to the counter. I had a plate of biscuits and gravy for Brad with a side of fluffy scrambled eggs. It had only taken me half a carton of eggs to get them right, but I'd done it.

Brad was finished making the coffee

and had returned to his spot next to Zoey.

Zoey tapped her fork on her very clean-looking plate. "Hey, can I get another order to-go? I haven't been to bed yet. This would be perfect for when I wake up."

"You sure? I was planning on making steak hoagies again for lunch. Give me a text when you wake up and I can run one over."

"You're getting in a lot of practice there with those steaks. When are you going to go all the way and serve up some steak dinners?" Zoey asked.

I scrunched my face. "I'm having trouble getting the cook right. I've been watching a bunch of cooking shows on my cell phone, and it seems like steaks are like martinis. Everybody likes them made a very specific way, and they get unhappy when you don't get it right. I need more practice."

Brad shrugged. "You can come over. We'll practice together." I felt my cheeks heat and knew I was blushing. "You ever grilled over an open flame? We could even do some that way."

"Grill? Outside? But it's been so cold."

"All the better. Easier to deal with standing next to the grill." He smiled, and I lost myself for a moment in how incredibly handsome he was. I couldn't believe he wanted to spend time with me. I mean, of course he wanted to spend time with me. He was at the café every morning. But he was wanting to spend time with me outside the café, too. He was wanting to take things to the next level.

Butterflies took flight in my stomach.

The last man I'd had a serious relationship with had lied to me through nine years of marriage. He'd played me like a fool, and for eight and a half years of that marriage, I believed everything he'd said.

Now I had two men—Brad and Joel—who were interested in exploring a relationship. I wasn't sure I was ready. I wasn't sure I'd ever be ready.

"Brad—"

"That's my cue," Zoey said, getting off her stool and plopping thirty onto the counter. "This is for breakfast and lunch. I'm outta here. Remember to send over that steak hoagie later… And some more biscuits and gravy. I want 'em both." How was the girl so skinny? I didn't know where she put it all. "I'll text you when I'm ready to, you know…" She made a circular motion with her finger in the air. I knew what she was saying. She was saying that she'd let me know when she was ready to go out to further investigate Mike's death.

"What? What's this?" Brad said, duplicating Zoey's twirling finger. "What are you two up to? I'm not going to like it, am I? I should incarcerate Zoey just to split the two of you up. You're trouble together."

"Eat your breakfast, old man," Zoey said, giving him a friend-pat on the shoulder.

"Old? I'm three years older than you," Brad complained.

And that made him four years younger than me. Brad and Zoey were young, but I'd never felt older in my life.

Dan was nine years older than me. I'd always been the youthful one, the forever-young one.

I glanced over at Agatha and Conrad. I wasn't sure how many years there were between them, but the age difference was more than mine, Brad's and Zoey's age differences combined, and it didn't faze Agatha or Conrad one bit. They were totally smitten with each other. Everything else was irrelevant, just a number.

That was only one of several life lessons I needed to take from Agatha. Figuring out how to live life in the moment was at the top of my list.

I turned to Brad. "I'd love to make steaks with you. Just name the night."

CHAPTER 21

I'd barely gotten done tapping on Zoey's apartment door with the toe of my sneaker when the door jerked open. I had a bag of biscuits and a container of gravy in one arm and two wrapped plates bearing steak hoagies and coleslaw in the other. It was after three PM, and I'd left Sam in charge of the café with instructions for heating up baked spaghetti and meatballs that I'd prepped that morning. He'd have plenty of food to feed the dinner crowd, not that I expected very many customers. It was Sunday, and we were running out of the magical cookie dough that had lured so many new customers in.

"Those both for me?" Zoey asked, looking at the double hoagies.

"One for me, one for you."

"Cool. Gimme," she said, rescuing the plates from where they teetered on my arm and against my stomach.

We sat in our usual spots on her living room floor on top of oversized comfy cushions. I watched as she opened her steak hoagie and scooped the side dish of coleslaw inside of it.

"What are you doing?" I asked.

"Eating." She took a huge bite of the now overstuffed hoagie.

"Any good that way?"

"Oh, yeah. It's a thing. People do this."

"People do that?"

"Yeah, didn't you know? I thought that was why you made coleslaw."

"No," I said, dumbfounded that I'd stumbled onto this new way of eating coleslaw.

"You gotta do it."

I opened my hoagie, piled in the coleslaw and then did my best to balance the top back in place. I opened my mouth so wide that the hinges of my jaw ached, then I bit down. The bread was soft with a slight buttery crunch from where I'd toasted the inside of each slice. The steak was juicy, tender and flavorful. The sautéed sweet onions were sweet, the green peppers were delicate yet distinct, and the coleslaw was tangy, fresh and crisp. Together, it was amazing!

"Holy cow," I said with my mouth still stuff full of food.

"See, what'd I tell ya," Zoey said, smiling.

I hadn't noticed anyone in the café eating the steak hoagies this way. Of course, today was the first day that I'd made them with a side of coleslaw. This dish was definitely ready to come off the Oops Board, and I would even add the option of preloading the sandwich with the coleslaw.

We ate in silence for a while until Zoey asked, "We got a plan?"

"I say we go back and talk to Clara some more. She's up to something."

Zoey narrowed her eyes. "You're jealous."

"I am not," I said with such vehemence that some particles of food actually took flight. I shut my mouth and chewed sullenly.

"No, you are. You're jealous that her café is going so well."

I shifted positions, stretching my legs out in front of me. There was no use hiding my feelings from Zoey. She could see right through any bluster. "Did you see how much she charges? It's insane. But she had all those customers! I don't get it. I don't charge half of what she does and until those cookies, I struggled to get anybody in the door."

"You did almost murder somebody," Zoey said.

"So did you," I shot back.

We both knew that wasn't true. Neither one of us had killed anyone, not that the townspeople necessarily believed that. To some, we were guilty. It didn't matter that we'd been cleared by the law.

"Helps keep people in line," Zoey said

with a satisfied smirk. "Some jerk started to overcharge me for car maintenance. I gave him one look and he caved. Admitted that there might not be anything wrong with my carburetor."

"Huh! Wish that had worked on Lou Sizemore, the guy who's fixing the boiler. He wasn't intimidated at all."

"How's that going?" Zoey asked. "Gonna have it working again soon?"

"I don't know. I heard that the old one busted when they were moving it out of the building and it flooded everything down there. They couldn't work in it because of electrocution concerns until they sump pumped it dry. The flooding and cleanup exposed a crack in the building's foundation, and it's going to be another five thousand dollars to fix it." I shook my head. "I'm going to be ruined at this rate."

"It'll get better," Zoey said.

"You're just saying that," I groused.

"True."

We finished our food and headed out. When we arrived at *The Java Hole,* Susie's shop next door had its lights off and a Closed sign in the door.

Not unusual for a Sunday evening, Kylie thought to herself. But the hair salon of Susie's arch nemesis, Betty, was open for business and looked as if it had customers inside.

"So, Susie's shop is struggling but Clara's and Betty's isn't," I said.

"We don't know that yet. Clara's coffee shop could be empty."

I leaned a little to get an inconspicuous peek through the glass front windows. Her place was half full. Everybody had a drink at their table and most had a small plate that featured some treat or other. Knowing how high Clara's rates were, I said dourly, "She's doing fine."

We headed in. Clara was behind the barista counter wearing a cotton blouse that was loose but gossamer thin. Its free-flowing fabric seemed to want to hug itself to her slender frame all on its own. It was a shirt choice that one could claim was demure and understated, yet when worn it was anything but. And it irked me. Her shirt's dual identity was just like her personality. She was a person who liked to proclaim to the world that she was a good and gentle soul, but in reality she was a beautiful, graceful snake that would strike without regret if annoyed.

Clara spotted us when we got three quarters of the way to her. "Stop," she said, holding up her hand. "If you two are here to ask more questions, you can turn yourselves right back around and leave."

"We only have one question," I reassured her.

"Yeah, and what's that?"

Zoey delivered the punch. "We want to know when your affair with Mike Pratt started."

We'd opted to ask when it started as the safest bet. If Clara had had an affair with Mike, that affair could have been ongoing or it could have ended ages ago. But regardless of the affair's status and whether or not it had ended prior to Mike's death, if one existed, there would have been a start date.

In truth, we had no idea if Clara had

had an affair with Mike. But given what Susie had told us—that Clara would flirt with Mike and that he'd seemed charmed by her—it was certainly possible that the two had shared more than what either had made public.

"Well I never!" Clara said, indignant.

"We think you have," Zoey said.

Clara's indignation shifted to venomous ire, and I wondered how Clara would manage to slip a laxative into Zoey's coffee. "Well it doesn't matter what you think, now does it? Mike is dead and buried in the ground. Whatever you think was between us—which was *nothing*—doesn't matter."

"Unless it happened to matter to whoever killed him," I said.

Clara's mouth opened and shut several times before she found her words again. "Are you insinuating that *I* killed Mike?" Again, she'd called him by his first name only. It was a very personal thing to do, and it belied a relationship that was more casual than others had felt that they had with him. For instance, Susie tended to call him Mr. Pratt. She didn't use his first name at all, instead staying very formal.

Zoey shrugged. "We wouldn't blame you. We're sure you had your reasons. Was he sleeping around on you?"

"No, he wasn't sleeping around on me!"

"So he was faithful to you?" Zoey asked.

"No... no. Stop putting words in my mouth. Mike and I were not and never had been in a relationship."

Zoey and I looked at each other, then I said, "Well, a relationship... We didn't ask you about a *relationship*. We'd asked if you were having an affair."

"You two are the worst. Why hasn't someone killed you yet? Half the town would get together and have a party. I'd host... I did not kill Mike. I did not have an affair or a relationship with him. If you want to know who killed Mike, then you need to start paying closer attention to your girl Susie and spend less time trying to pin Mike's murder on somebody else. And his neighbor! My God! That creepy little ghost of a woman. There is something wrong with her! She's *weird.* Why aren't you at her house, harassing her? And what about Mae, next door to me? Why aren't you grilling her? What's so special about me?"

"I don't like you, but I respect you," Zoey said.

"Huh?" Clara said, and I almost said it with her.

"When somebody wrongs you, you do something about it. You take action. You make them pay a price."

Ohhhh, right! I jumped in. "You accosted one of your customers."

"I did no such thing." Indignant Clara was back.

"You drugged her drink."

Clara looked confused.

Zoey spelled it out. "You put Ex-lax in her coffee."

Clara's confusion was instantly replaced with amusement, but then she seemed to remember who she was talking to. "You can't prove anything."

It was my turn. "There were witnesses. And you called the police on her and her husband when they rushed out without paying. There would be a police report. I'm sure that the couple had a lot to say when the police caught up with them."

Clara scowled and slouched a little.

"Then there was Terrance, at the *Saucy Dog*." Zoey said. "He stole one of your waitresses. You went in during the busiest part of his day and claimed that he'd given you food poisoning. Told him you'd put him out of business if he ever tried to steal one of your waitresses again."

"So. What?" Clara did not look impressed.

"The so what," I said, "is that you like your vengeance. Mike died… Someone took vengeance on him. Forgive me if I'm wrong, but I'm seeing a pattern here."

Clara leaned forward, and her voice lowered. "If you're seeing a pattern, then where are the cops? They're not here, 'cause you got nothing. Now get out of my shop before I do decide to do something to you."

When we got back outside into the cold, early evening air, I asked, "Think she did it?"

"I don't know. Maybe. But we need to go talk to Mike's neighbor."

"I agree, but I want to talk to Betty first." Her beauty salon was nearly directly across from where we were standing. She would have been able to see everything that happened on this side of the street. I had a hunch that she held our next clue.

CHAPTER 22

The door of *Betty's Beauties* chimed as Zoey and I stepped inside. There was easy listening music playing with the volume low and the gentle burbling of a waterfall in the corner. Live plants gave warmth and life to the place, and it smelled of apples and cinnamon. Everything about the salon was tasteful, and no part of the salon's welcoming features overwhelmed any of the others.

There were three beauticians working. The nearest had thick black hair with a vivid strand of blue and a couple of strands of white weaving through it, all pulled up into a messy up-do that looked good on the thirty-something woman. She had a body reminiscent of a Grecian goddess—a voluptuous softness and grace.

Across the room from her were two other beauticians, both with wicker privacy barriers that gave them their own private space. They didn't have a clear view of each other, the rest of the shop or what was going on outside beyond the shop's glass front windows. But the black-haired lady could see everything. She could see who walked in, what the other beauticians were doing, and she had a clear view out the front of the shop.

It was my guess that she was the illustrious Betty, customer thief and archrival of Susie. I didn't want to like her or her shop, yet I instantly did. This woman was on top of her game. Her salon was lovely, inviting and relaxing. I could already feel the tension draining away from my shoulders. If Susie weren't my friend, I'd want to come to get my hair done in

Betty's salon just for the chance to sit in its quiet tranquility.

"I'll be right with you," the black-haired lady said. Her customer handed over some money, then got up out of her chair and gave the woman a hug. She was obviously happy with the service she'd gotten. I was pretty sure I'd never gotten a random hug from a customer, and I had to say it made me a little jealous. This woman seemed to have life all figured out, and I instantly wanted to be her when I grew up.

The customer smiled as she walked past us and out the door. We were standing in the salon's front lobby area. There were a couple of coffee tables strewn with a wide collection of hairstyle books and magazines, and it was the only area of the salon that was covered in carpet instead of white tile.

"What can I do for you ladies?" the black-haired woman asked with a smile as she came to where we stood.

"Are you Betty?" I asked. It really

didn't matter if she was Betty or not. Her work station had a clear view of everything across the street. She was definitely the person we wanted to speak to.

"I am," she said, and that was a relief. If we were talking with the owner of the shop, she wouldn't have a boss looking over her shoulder and telling her to get back to work.

"We were hoping to have a few minutes to talk to you," I said.

"Oh!" Betty blinked, but then followed up with a disarming and charming smile. "That sounds so ominous, but you two get comfortable"—she waved toward the thickly cushioned chairs near one of the coffee tables—"and I'll be right back."

Without waiting for a reply, she disappeared into a room at the back of the shop. Zoey and I got comfortable. We didn't have to wait long. Almost as quickly as Betty had gone into the back room, she was back, carrying a tray with her. She set it down on the coffee table. On it were delicious looking finger sandwiches—I guessed cream cheese and cucumber—and a couple of cans of ice cold soda.

Not wanting to offend her sense of hospitality, I picked up a soda and handed it to Zoey before getting one for myself. Then I got one of the finger sandwiches. I bit into it and then groaned. What I'd thought was a simple sandwich of cream cheese and cucumbers actually had hints of dill and garlic.

"Oh my God, these are so good!" Was everyone a better cook than me? Okay… I was better off not answering that question.

"Oh, you're too kind," Betty said, giving me a beauty contestant smile. "But I must know, you have me so curious. What is it that you're wanting to talk to me about?"

I suddenly felt awkward. I liked this woman, and I immediately felt myself looking up to her as a possible mentor. She was so vibrant and strong, a successful business owner, a person who understood the value of customer relations. I didn't feel comfortable picking through her brain to see what dirt she knew. It felt debasing.

I glanced over at Zoey, and Zoey gave a nod, understanding that I wanted her to take the lead.

"Did you know Mike Pratt?" Zoey asked.

"Why, sure. All of us shop owners around here knew Mike." Her face grew long. "So sad about what happened to him."

"Do you happen to remember anything about the day he died?"

"Hmm, that was what? Last Monday? Let's see..." She took a moment to think. "I had a perm, three haircuts, a color and a hair consultation. Renee had mostly cuts, and Jenny had cuts and a late perm."

"Good memory," I said. It was an excellent sign. If there was anything else memorable about the day, there was a good chance that she'd be able to recall it. "Do you happen to remember anything else about the day? Do you remember by any chance Susie or Clara leaving their shops?" Per her own words, we already knew that Susie had left her shop, twice. She'd gone over to see Mike at his home office. They'd had a fight, she'd left, and then she'd gone back again. It was when she'd gone back again that she'd found Mike dead.

"Mmm, nooo… I don't recall her coming and going. Oh," she chuckled, "but there was that huge fight between her and Mike out in front of her place." Her face lost its humor. "Well, I found it funny at the time. I guess in retrospect, given what happened to Mike only an hour or two later, maybe it's not so funny."

"What?" This was news to me. Susie hadn't said anything about it. "Susie and Mike had a fight on Monday?"

"Mmhmm, right out in front of her salon. I guess she probably had somebody in the chair or else why take such a thing outdoors, but they did. Susie wasn't even wearing a coat. She was just standing out there in the cold, waving her arms around and yelling."

"You could hear them?" Zoey asked.

"Nooo," she said, drawing the word out.

"Then how do you know that Susie was yelling?"

"Well, it was her body language! She had her hands up in the air"—Betty demonstrated by lifting her arms so that her hands were up near her head—"and she was leaning forward real aggressive like. It was obvious. She was yelling. Poor girl."

"You felt sorry for her?" I asked, surprised. According to Susie, Betty had aggressively campaigned to steal her clients away. She'd made up stories that Susie had left someone with bald patches and had ruined people's hair.

Remembering who I was talking to, my instant like of her started to dim.

"Oh, yes! When she opened her shop right across from mine, I thought, well good for you! You go girl! But, this is a demanding profession." She shook her head, her face sad. "It's not for everyone. And, well, some people peak in high school and then spend the whole rest of their lives coming to terms that they've already seen the best they're ever going to be."

Oh… burn. I could almost feel the dagger sinking into Susie's back myself. I hadn't even seen it coming until Betty was sliding it in. She was good!

"Do you have any idea what the fight between her and Mike was about?" Zoey asked.

"No, I don't. I'm sorry."

"What happened next?" I asked.

"Well, Susie was out there yelling and waving her arms—bless her heart—and Mike just turned around and walked away. Just like that. Turned around and left her yelling in the street."

"What'd they do?" I asked.

"Mike, he went on into Clara's place, and Susie stood outside her place for about a minute, staring where Mike had been, and then finally stomped off inside her own place. Oh! And then, after Mike came out of Clara's place, he went into Mae's florist shop. Why, when he came out his arms were plum full of long-stem roses!" Her eyes twinkled. "I wonder what lucky girl got those." Then as if remembering what had happened to Mike a little while later, she said, "I mean, you know, if anyone had the chance to get them."

Long-stem roses were expensive. Really expensive. Mike wasn't known for being a generous person, at least not unless he was taking some almost-too-young beauty on a country-hopping vacation. We still had no idea who Mike was involved with, if anyone. But him buying roses certainly did lend credence to the idea that he did have a special someone in his life.

I didn't have proof that there wasn't a romantic relationship between Mike and Susie, but I also had heard absolutely nothing to support that idea. In contrast, Susie had said that Clara would practically hang off the man's arm and would have him blushing like a school girl.

"Do you have any idea who the roses might have been for?" I asked.

"Could have been Tina—she is… was his neighbor."

My mouth almost fell open. Clara had talked Tina up like she was a total loon. Here Betty was talking about Tina as a possible romantic partner of Mike's.

"What makes you think that?" I asked.

"Oh, I don't know." She waved a hand dismissively. "You pick up things, tidbits. I mean, yeah, Tina's an odd duck. Honestly, she's a little stalkerish if you ask me. I did her hair a few times, and Mike was all she would talk about. I'd change the subject, and she'd go right back to talking about him. Obsessed, I'm tellin' you. The girl was two steps away from needing psychiatric care or an intervention, if you ask me. Oh, and jealous! My word. She mentioned something about getting wind that Mike had taken someone out on a couple of dates, so this girl stalks her, night and day."

"She told you that?" It was hard to

believe that someone would tell something like that on themselves.

"Oh, honey!" Betty laughed. "Owning a salon has its perks. People get in that chair and it's like they got injected with truth serum. It alll comes out." She laughed again. "I know who's having an affair with who, who got busted for DUI, who's been hitting their wives, who's addicted to painkillers, who's selling painkillers, and who's got a bag packed with plans to leave it all behind. Sweetie, I know more than the cops do. They've got nothin' on me. This place is like grapevine central. Everybody tells everything in here." She shrugged. "It feels like a safe space. And it is. This is where people can come to get away from their lives, their worries and their problems, if even for a little while. It's what I give back to the community. It's my contribution."

Her gaze became unfocused as she looked past Zoey and me where we sat in front of the windows. I turned around a looked. Clara was crossing the street, a to-go cup in each hand. We were about to get interrupted, and this little heart-to-heart was about to end. I had to hurry if I wanted to learn anything else.

"Is there anything you can tell us about Clara?" I asked.

Betty made a face, kind of like she'd bitten into a lemon. But she didn't offer up any words.

"You don't like her?" I pressed.

"Well, like... it's such a grade school thing to say." She shrugged. "Clara's okay. Not very trustworthy, but okay."

"Not trustworthy?"

"Life is hard. It's a dog-eat-dog world, and Clara's not willing to be a victim. I can respect that." Then she hedged, cringing. "But she can be a bit heavy-handed in her reactions. If she feels an offense, she'll cut your throat. Metaphorically speaking, of course."

"Of course," I said, not convinced. We had maybe seconds left. I spoke quickly. "Do you think she could have killed Mike?"

"Clara? Noooo. Clara's got a temper."

I was failing to see how that was

making an argument in her defense. "And?"

"And... you don't go through life with a temper like hers and not have a rap sheet ten miles long if you don't know how to manage yourself. No, Clara wouldn't have done it. She's too self-serving. Facing prison for murder would not be something she'd be interested in risking."

"And what about Susie?" Zoey asked.

Betty burst out in laughter, like she'd just heard the punch line of an unexpected joke. "That girl's a titmouse. Doesn't have it in her. She's... well, like I said, bless her heart, she just doesn't have the backbone to stand up to someone like Mike Pratt."

The door chimed. Without looking, I knew that Clara had arrived.

"You two digging up more dirt on me?" Clara asked drolly. Without saying anything directly to Betty, she handed her the to-go cup of what I assumed was coffee that she carried in her hand.

"These two are awful," she said to Betty. "You should kick them out."

Betty laughed. "Clara, be nice," she chided. "Here, have one of these and tell me what you think." She picked up the plate of finger sandwiches and held it out to Clara. Clara took one, took a bite, and her brows went up.

"Very nice!" she said. "Where'd you get the recipe?"

"I thought you might like those," Betty said, smiling and as at ease as she was the first moment we'd seen her.

Zoey and I stood. It was clear that we wouldn't be learning anything more.

"Mmmm, you two giving up trying to clear Susie's of murder and pin it on me instead?" Clara goaded as we headed for the door. "Don't stop on my account. By all means, you must save your precious Susie!"

I was going to say something to placate Clara, but Zoey spoke first, and she spoke to me.

"Let's go get some coffee. Yours is so much better than anywhere else."

Clara's hand tightened around her cup so hard that the lid popped off and the contents sloshed out. She hissed as it burned her hand.

Zoey looked her up and down. "Couldn't have happened to a better person."

CHAPTER 23

Zoey pulled into Mike Pratt's driveway and parked. Knowing that Mike was dead and that his house was empty gave it an ominous, sentient appearance. The sky was overcast with what looked like heavy snow clouds, and night was on its way.

On one side of Mike's home was the park where the four homeless people had been living. On the other side was a ranch-style home a little smaller than Mike's, and it was owned by Mike's infamous neighbor.

"Think Tina's home?" I asked.

"Her curtains moved. She's home."

For some reason, knowing that she

was over there peering at us from out of sight made me feel exposed. It didn't matter that we hadn't even gotten out of Zoey's car yet.

"What do you think we should do first, check for the homeless people first or talk to Tina?"

"Homeless people," Zoey said. "If things get weird with Tina—and everybody says it will—could get awkward heading next door to the park afterward. If she turned homicidal on us, it would leave us exposed as well."

Good points.

We got out of the car and headed into the park. There was a run-walk path covered with what looked like shredded bark. There were a few park benches beneath a tree big enough to be seen from outer space. A tin-roofed, no wall shelter provided cover for a set of four picnic tables and what looked like an outdoor grill.

It wasn't a very big park, but it looked like it was loved. It was well cared for, even if it did look cold, stark and lonely in the gloomy winter light.

In addition to the other park features, sitting unobtrusively to the side was the small cinderblock building that offered his-hers bathroom options. It was the spot the four had turned into a makeshift home. And as makeshift homes went, I had to admit, one with running water, a solid roof, and built-in toilet facilities wasn't too bad. Definitely could be worse.

The small building looked deserted, but there was only one sure way to find out.

Zoey and I headed over. Zoey crinkled her nose when we got near. I couldn't smell anything, but maybe she could.

"I'll wait here," she said. "Guard against a surprise attack by Tina."

I wanted to believe that Zoey's comment was said fully in jest, but I wasn't sure it was.

I headed in. Choosing the ladies' side first, I called out softly, "Hello? Anybody home?" I didn't get an answer, and due diligence had my hand on the door to take a peek inside. Which is what I did.

There, to my horror, was a wrinkly old man naked from the waist down. He had a foot thrown over one of the sinks and the water was running.

I gasped, clenched my eyes shut and turned to go back out. But I misgauged where the door frame was and bashed the side of my head into it. That made me open my eyes, and I really wished I hadn't opened my eyes. I was no longer looking at the man's backside—I was looking at his frontside!

"Oh! No! I'm sorry!" I said, closing my eyes again and holding my hand up as if to further shield the old fellow from my sight.

"What in tarnation. Git. Git!"

I got. I stumbled and bounced my way back out of there, or at least I tried. Zoey charging in had us both scrambling and covering our eyes, tangled together and turning around in circles.

"Git! Git outta my home!"

We both forced our way out the door

at the same time. I almost went down on my knees, but Zoey caught me. "Open your eyes!"

"Oh yeah!" I'd forgotten that it was now safe to see. The old man was inside, behind inches and inches of concrete block. But that did nothing for the image of him seared onto my retina. I grabbed Zoey by her shoulders. "I can't unsee it, Zoey. I can't unsee it."

Zoey thunked me—hard—with the flick of her middle finger on my forehead.

"Hey!" I jerked back and rubbed the spot she hit.

"Not thinking about him anymore, are ya?"

"Well I am now," I complained, but she was right. Somehow she always knew how to put things in perspective.

The door to the ladies' bathroom opened and the old man emerged. Thankfully, he was clothed on both his upper half… and his lower half. "Can a man bathe himself without hooligans like you barging in where ye ain't wanted?"

He was incredibly bowlegged. His feet

were maybe six inches apart from one another, but his knees looked more like a full twelve inches apart. He had a dark gray toboggan on his head and a thickly padded, oversized tan coat wrapped around his torso. His pants looked as though they might have once been considered business slacks, and his shoes were sneakers, one of which had a little help from duct tape.

"Hygiene, that's what these johnny-come-latelies don't get. It's hygiene. It'll make or break you out here."

I studied the man a little more closely. He was somewhere between sixty and ninety, was roughly five-foot eight, and had the hair of a man marooned on a deserted island for the last twenty years. His hair was a mix of dark gray and white, and his scraggly beard looked as though it could double as a bird's nest.

But… he looked clean. Even his clothes.

"I'm sorry. I'm so sorry," I said. "I didn't mean to disturb you. I was looking for the people who were staying here before you."

"Before me? Before me! That riffraff moved in on my place two months ago when I was out collecting cans. I got back home—to *my* home," he said, jabbing his thumb into his chest, "and they wouldn't give it up. But now I finally got it back, and *you ain't takin' it!*"

I waved my hands in front of me. "No, sir. We don't want it. I promise. I'm sorry that you lost your home, and I'm happy that you've gotten it back, but do you know by any chance where the people who had been staying here have gone?"

"Don't know. Don't care."

I wanted to scream in frustration. I was never going to find out who made those cookies! And, my little café had never done so well. I needed those cookies. It could mean the difference between being able to keep everything or losing it all by going financially under.

"Old man," Zoey said, shifting her hip bag, "you said you used to live here until up to two months ago. How long did you live here?"

The old guy shuffled his feet like he didn't want to answer.

"We're not going to tell anyone," Zoey said.

"I've lived here for a couple of years. Yeah, I gotta clear all my stuff out during the good months, months when people come here. I take all my stuff out so it don't get in anybody's way and so they won't call anybody on me, then when everybody's gone for the night, I move my stuff back in."

"Where do you go when you move your stuff out?"

"Sometimes I go get something to eat down at the mission. Sometimes I hang out here." He stood up straighter. "Because I'm clean, people don't avoid me so much. They're friendly. In the summer, almost every day somebody's out here grilling or having a picnic, and they almost always offer me a plate, too." There was pride in his voice.

Guilt filled me. It wasn't summer,

spring or fall, and every time we'd been out here to check this park for my phantom cookie maker, it had been empty. I wondered when it was that the old man had last had a hot meal... or any meal.

Zoey must have been having similar thoughts because she spoke up. "We could take you to the shelter. Get you out of the cold."

The old guy shifted, planting his feet. "I ain't leavin' my home." Then he seemed to mellow. "And I sleep good and warm. I got a sleeping bag and I wrap myself in one of those tinfoil like space blankets and then get in that bag. I put another space blanket around my head. Little babies don't sleep as good."

"Did you know the guy who lived here?" Zoey asked, pointing behind us toward Mike's house with her thumb.

The old guy looked past us before he focused on Zoey again. "I told ya. I weren't here. Them others were here. Not me. I didn't do it."

"So you know he's dead?" Zoey asked with all the tact of a Sherman tank.

"Yeah, it's what I heard."

"Did you know him?"

"I kept to myself. He didn't call no one on me." He shuffled his feet. "I guess that made him an okay guy."

There was something about the way that he said it that made me need to ask. "Was he not an okay guy otherwise?"

"He had himself a lot of ladies. Always comin' and goin', those ladies. Didn't respect 'em, though."

"What makes you say that?"

"Well! It's like I said, all them ladies, comin' and goin'. If you got a revolving door on your love life, you're not treatin' somebody right."

That logic sounded spot on to me. The old guy had a clue or two about life, which of course made me wonder what had led him to be here, on his own.

"Do you know the lady who lives next door to this house?" Zoey asked.

He scowled. "She's a funny one."

Wow. It was unanimous. Every single

person we'd asked about Tina had described her as being someone outside the norm.

"How's she funny?"

The old guy narrowed his eyes. "Is harassing old men the only thing you got to do?"

"We could just call someone," Zoey said, pulling her cell phone out of her pocket. "The cops maybe?"

"Now, now. No reason to get testy on me. Put that thing away. I'll tell ya what you want to know."

Zoey put the phone away. "I'm listening."

The old guy cleared his throat. "What is it you're wantin' to know?"

Zoey pointed over her shoulder again. "The lady living in that house. What can you tell us about her?"

The old guy shrugged. "I can tell you that she was one of them ladies goin' through Mr. Pratt's revolving door."

I needed to clarify. "You're saying that Tina—the lady who lives in that house—and Mike Pratt were having an affair."

"Mmm, used to be that way. Not so sure anymore."

Mike was dead and buried in the ground. I sure hoped there wasn't an anymore.

"How recent?" Zoey asked.

The guy shrugged his shoulders. "Not sure. I think maybe they were on again, off again. I see her creepin'."

"Creepin'?" I asked.

"Yeah, she'd go over to his place in the middle of the night wearing nothing but one of them shiny, short nighties. Sometimes but not so often, I'd see Mr. Pratt leaving her place right when the sun was coming up. They'd carry on for a while, then Mike's girls would start back up, then him and the neighbor lady would be going back and forth, then Mike's girls would be back again. Don't know if they were creepin' when he got himself choked."

As risqué as all that was, that didn't qualify Tina as a "funny one."

"Why don't you like Tina?" I asked.

"Never said I didn't like her."

Zoey saved me, understanding what I was trying to ask. "How's she odd?"

"Oh," he shrugged. He thought a moment. "Ever been called to the principal's office, then sat there in front of his desk while he stared at you without saying a word?"

I hadn't, but I nodded my head anyway.

"It's like that."

"Huh," Zoey said, sounding as though she knew exactly what the ol' guy was saying. "Thank you for your time. We'll let you get back to your…" She wagged a finger at him and let her sentence trail off.

"Have you had dinner?" I asked, blurting out the question. I saw Zoey roll her eyes in the corner of my vision.

"Vienna sausages out of a can." He looked at me speculatively. "You got somethin' better?"

"I might. I could send somebody by with some baked spaghetti meatballs."

"Cold… or hot?"

"Hot. Good and hot. I could send some hot coffee, too."

The old guy blew out a breath. "Coffee." The word was said with pure reverence, and I knew I'd found somebody I could help.

"I don't have a thermos—"

"I do. I got a thermos," the old guy said, cutting me off. "I could get it for ya. It's clean!"

I smiled. "That'd be great." The old man had made me a happy girl. I was going to get the chance to feed someone for whom a good, hot meal really mattered. I was a happy girl indeed.

CHAPTER 24

"You can't keep him," Zoey said. Her expression was impassive.

"What?" I was playing dumb.

Zoey remained impassive.

"I wasn't going to keep him."

Still impassive.

"I wasn't."

No emotion whatsoever.

"Ahh, come on! He's so sweet!"

"He's been alive a long time. He's got baggage. You don't need his baggage. You've got your own baggage."

"But Henry's so cute," I whined.

"See, now you've named him. You're getting attached already."

We were walking across the yard of Mike Pratt's house on our way to his neighbor's house. I had Henry's thermos tucked under my arm, and as promised, it was clean. I'd send Sam back with a big plate of food and a thermos of hot coffee later. It was a bit outside his job description, but I didn't think he'd mind.

Together, Zoey and I stepped over a low-growing hedge that marked what I assumed was the boundary of Mike's property and the beginning of his neighbor's property. The grass was brown from the hard freezes of late, but despite that, her yard was immaculate. It was landscaped with defined areas of mulch and stone that I was sure would sport colorful flowers in the spring.

The house was well-kept, too. The ornamental shutters on the windows were painted a vivid blue, a color that popped against the soft, delicate pastel of the house. Between the care given to the house and the yard, I could easily imagine it gracing the cover of a beautiful-homes magazine.

We reached her burgundy-brown front door. It had a narrow windowpane on each side, with a frosted, swirling designed etched into the glass.

Zoey knocked.

No answer. No sound from within, but I thought that I saw a shadow move from somewhere deep inside the house through the side window.

Zoey knocked again.

No answer. No anything.

"I think she's stonewalling us," I said. I lifted my closed fist with my knuckles poised to bang on the glass rather than the door, then screamed and jerked my hand back in surprise when a woman's face materialized right at the spot where I'd been about to knock. Her eyes bulged out of her round little face. She looked like a pug.

The infamous Tina, no doubt. True to everyone's word, just from looking at her, I got the impression she was odd.

She opened her door and wedged herself into the space between the frame and the door itself. Her body was small and lithe, like that of a teenage ballerina, but her face wore the miles of her worried, harried life—whether those worries were imagined or otherwise. As for the rest of her, she wore jeans and a plain green V-neck.

"What do you want?" she asked. She spoke fast enough to gain the respect of a high-speed narrator, maybe even an auctioneer. It was unnerving, and completely threw me off guard. Everything about her felt aggressive.

"We want to know how long your affair with Mike lasted," Zoey said.

"You don't know what you're talking about." Again with the lightning-speed speech.

It was my turn to find my voice. "We have an eye witness. You and Mike were having an affair."

"I don't know who you are or why you're talking to me. Go away." She tried to close her door, but Zoey wedged her booted foot against it. Tina looked down at Zoey's foot, then up at her. "I'll call the police. You killed that guy a few weeks ago. You tased him. Now you're harassing me. You'll go to jail."

Zoey moved her foot and Tina started to slam her door shut, but instead it met with the sudden, explosive resistance of Zoey's boot slamming into it. The door flew open all the way, and Zoey took her taser from her hip bag. Blue sparks shot between the tips of its two metal prongs. "He didn't die from my taser. I'll show you." Zoey extended her arm, and Tina jumped back, leaving her doorway completely vacant and open.

Zoey walked in, and I followed, closing the door behind us. My brain was doing mental acrobatics trying to figure out if what just happened would be considered breaking and entering, or at the very least unlawful entry.

"I'll call the police," Tina said again, but she wasn't making any moved to do so.

I looked at Zoey. "I don't think they were planning on picking her up until tomorrow, but I'm sure they wouldn't mind moving up their schedule."

"Picking me up? What are you saying? What are you talking about?" We had Tina's attention, and she was finally on the defensive instead of the offensive. We had the upper hand.

"The police," I said, "they're coming for you tomorrow. They found your fingerprints all over Mike's house." If Tina had had an affair with Mike at some point, it made sense that she would have left fingerprints at his house.

"You're lying. That's a lie. A big, fat lie. The police don't know anything."

Zoey pounced. "Don't know what, Tina?"

"Nothing, because there's nothing to know."

It was my turn again. "That's not what their witness said. Their witness said that there was a lot to know."

"There's nothing to know!" Tina shouted.

I kept my voice calm, level and soft. "When did things sour between you and Mike? When did you stop getting along?"

"You don't know anything!" Tina shouted again.

"Then tell us," I urged. "If we're getting it all wrong, then set the record straight. Tell us what it is that we don't know. Tell us about how he died."

"He was strangled. By his shredding machine. An accident."

Zoey's turn. "Then you didn't mean for it to happen?"

"Mean for it to happen? I wasn't even there! Why aren't you talking to one of those skanks he hooks up with?"

"But that was you," I said. "Mike was hooking up with you." I honestly thought she was going to hit me after those words left my mouth. I thought she was going to launch herself from where she stood and fly across the foyer to rip my eyes out. Her eyes were practically rotating in her head. There was a spot of spittle on her lip. She was unhinged.

To my surprise, rather than attack me, Tina spoke, and her speech slowed immensely. The words sounded breathy, like they were a struggle to harness to do the bidding of her mouth. "Not anymore. Not for months. He was a man whore. Worthless. Useless. A man whore."

"Do you know who he was seeing at the time of his death?" I asked.

"I wouldn't know."

Zoey crossed her arms, the taser still in hand. "You're the liar. You kept tabs on him. Watched every move he made. You knew everyone who came and left his house. That means that if you can't name the person who was here when he died, then that person was you."

"No," Tina declared. "It wasn't me."

"Then talk," I said. "Give us something we can use."

"Why are you here? You two ain't even cops."

"Consider us concerned citizens," Zoey said. "Now talk."

Tina's bulging eyes somehow managed to squint and her lips became nothing more than a thin line. "He slept with all his female tenants. He bragged to me once that he was nice to the ones that were nice to him, a scratch my back and I'll scratch yours type of thing. When they stopped scratching his back, he'd mess with 'em."

"Mess with them how?" I asked.

"He'd make life hard on them. He'd mess around with their contracts, push to see how much money he could get from them. He'd make a game of it, see how fast he'd get them to move out. If they moved out, he could get someone new in, someone to scratch his back."

I felt a little sick. I felt like I wanted to high five whoever it was who had shoved that scarf of his into his shredder and killed him.

"And if they wouldn't scratch his back at all?" I asked.

Tina shrugged. "He'd make their life miserable."

Zoey spoke up. "But he rented to some men, too, didn't he?"

"Yeah. Said it provided stability of income or something like that. He didn't mess with their contracts unless they started annoying him by complaining about needing maintenance to the property."

"You knew this? And you had an affair with him?" I didn't know why I was pointing an accusatory finger at her. Why should I hold her to blame for things her one-time lover had done?

Tina shrugged again. "He was charming." I looked at her dumbfounded. "Really charming. He made me happy. Made me feel like a princess."

"What went wrong?" I asked. I was afraid to know. I imagined him driving a dump truck up to her front door and unloading an entire load of doggie droppings as a practical joke, not caring that he was the only one who thought it was funny. He sounded like that kind of guy.

Tina shoved both her hands deep into her front pockets. "He ended it."

"How?" I asked, suspicion flaring.

"He decided in his head that it was done but didn't tell me. Acted annoyed every time I talked to him. Acted inconvenienced. Then the girls started back up. Couldn't always tell who they were."

"Were any of them his tenants?" Zoey asked.

"Pretty sure. He started having them come at night and he kept his lights off. I put flood lights in my yard so I could see, but he kept painting over them. I aimed floodlights right at his house after that."

"What he do?" I asked.

"He offered to buy my house."

"Oh…"

"At a quarter of its value."

"Ohhhh…"

"He started slapping me with lawsuits. Dumb stuff. Stuff like for watering my flower garden and the water running onto his land. So I started calling the cops on him."

"What for?"

"Indecent exposure."

"He exposed himself to you?"

"He exposed himself to someone."

"Within the privacy of his house?" Zoey asked.

"No, to skanky women whores."

The conversation had officially looped back on itself.

"What properties did he own?" I asked.

"He had properties all over town. He liked to buy up sections."

I wasn't expecting that answer. That created a much larger scope for our investigation. Possibly too large.

"Did he have any favorite sections he liked to harass more than others?" Zoey asked.

"Yeah, the tenants on Brunt Street." That was where Susie's shop was.

"Who on that street rented from him?"

"I don't know. It's not like I knew all his business."

"Try," I encouraged.

"I seen both them hairdressers over here, that snooty lady with the coffee shop, the goody two shoes with the flower shop. Oh, and Grace, she'd been here a lot lately, but she didn't rent from him. She works at the gift shop out at the visitor's center."

"What color hair does she have?" I asked on a hunch.

"Dark brown."

"Thought you said you couldn't see who was coming and going from his house," Zoey said.

"People got car plates, don't they?" Tina countered. "He wasn't gonna beat me. Men like him need to be held accountable."

"What does that look like?" I asked.

"What look like?"

"Mike being held accountable."

"I reckon it looks like him being strangled with his own scarf," Tina said, her buggy eyes unflinching as she stared straight at us.

It was time for us to go. I reached for the door.

"Where were you the Monday morning that Mike died?" Zoey asked.

"Sleeping. Here."

"Sleeping? In the middle of the day?" Zoey challenged.

"The girls always came at night, so I slept during the day."

We didn't let her door hit us on the way out, and I walked a little fast moving away from her house than I had toward it.

"She's a loon," Zoey said. "She did it."

She certainly had been obsessed with Mike while he'd been alive. "I don't know. Sounds like Mike had a lot of people coming and going. Maybe it was one of his late night women… or their boyfriend or husband."

"Tina's got no alibi. She said Mike had to be held accountable, and she showed no remorse for his death. She's a vigilante psycho."

We got halfway across Tina's lawn before her sprinklers came on. The water smelled like fish, which meant we smelled like fish by the time we got done sprinting to the street. She'd had the water laced with fish fertilizer.

I glared back at Tina's house and saw a curtain move. She'd turned on the sprinklers on purpose.

The woman did like her vengeance. And maybe, just maybe, Mike had choked on it.

CHAPTER 25

I sank down lower into the steaming water of my tub. It was a hard-earned luxury that I was quickly becoming addicted to. I had my face smeared in cold cream, my hair knotted into a messy bun, and Sage perched on the rounded edge of the tub. She was sitting with her front paws tucked under her and her eyelids almost —but not quite—completely closed.

"Mmm, you tell it, girl," I said, envious of her. She was in the bliss that I was searching for. I touched her nose with the tip of one wet finger and was rewarded with the sound of her gentle purr echoing off the tile surfaces of the bathroom.

I closed my eyes and sank a little deeper into the water. My process for heating water up on the stove had gained efficiency, and it hadn't taken me as long to fill the tub tonight. But even after the long day and the labor of getting ready to relax once I'd been able to call it a night, my mind wouldn't rest. Everything-Tina kept playing over and over again in my head. Her uber-aggression. Her wild eyes. Her tommy gun-style of throwing accusations at anyone and everyone. And the unnerving sensation that she had a knife stashed behind her back with plans to pull it out and run at you.

If anyone was ready to snap, it was her. She was small, but the scarf-eating shredder could have provided a lot of the muscle necessary to overpower Mike during his final moments.

"Susie gets to Mike's house on Monday, for the first visit, not the second one," I said to Sage. "Susie and Mike have it out. Susie leaves. Tina walks over from next door to Mike's place. It takes her all of forty-five seconds to get there from her house, and nobody notices her make the trip. She goes inside. She and Mike argue. He tries to ignore her and go about his work. She grabs the end of his scarf and feeds it into the shredder. Mike tries to pull away, tries to turn the shredder of or unplug it, but she cups her hands behind his head and gives it all her weight to pull his head down until the shredder chokes him out."

Sage continued to purr but didn't open her eyes anymore.

"What? You don't like it?"

Sage made a half chirp, half meow but otherwise remained unchanged. I could tell she wasn't impressed with my theory.

"You know," I said, "sometimes the most obvious solution is the *actual* solution."

No luck. Sage was taking the high road and refusing to enter into the debate.

Sighing, I closed my eyes and did my best to adopt Sage's zen master technique. One minute passed. Two minutes. No luck. Sage's yogi impression kept getting superseded by Tina's speed talking, vigilante antics. She'd talked obsessively about all the women coming and going, and I let it all replay in my mind.

That's when I heard it. A jiggle. It was a familiar jiggle, one that I'd heard twice before.

Someone was at the fire escape window-door.

My eyes flew open and I stared at Sage staring at me. Then with a growl, Sage jumped off the edge of the bed and slinked her way out of the bathroom, moving fast and with her body mass low to the floor.

"Son of a biscuit maker!" I swore. I had never dreamed that my new home would become the Grand Central Station of break-in attempts when I'd moved into the second story apartment. But this time I wasn't scared. I was mad. Really mad.

Like Rambo coming up out of the water, I stood. I didn't have a towel handy, so I pulled my shower curtain off its hooks and wrapped its opaque length around me. Then, I grabbed up my comb… and flipped it around to its pointy end.

I was going to war…

~

"Indecent exposure? How does that even work? Wasn't she at home?" Jack asked from his spot at the grill's counter. Joel, Agatha and Zoey were sitting next to him, and Brad was standing next to me, behind the counter and in front of them. Everyone had a breakfast plate, but no one touched their food.

"Exactly—it's ridiculous!" Brad said, wiping a laughter tear from the corner of his eye. "So, the complaint comes into the station and I come over here to see what's what. Kylie had been in the tub when she heard someone jiggling her window. She gets out, wraps herself in her shower curtain, and goes running down the hall toward her window screaming like a banshee. Her feet get tangled in the shower curtain and she's either got to let it go to keep running or fall flat on her face in a heap of plastic."

"You know, I was there. You weren't. I should be the one telling this story," I said grumpily.

"But there's someone standing outside on her fire escape, so she keeps running," Brad continued, completely ignoring me. "Naked as a jaybird, waving a comb over her head and with cold cream all over her face."

There were looks of disbelief and awe on the faces of those sitting at the counter.

I glared. "Really! Do you have to repeat everything I told you? I was only that specific for the sake of your police report."

Absolutely no one cared what I had to say. Everyone's eyes were on Brad.

"So she drops the curtain but she's out of control, arms flailing, still trying not to fall," Brad said, fighting through his laughter.

"Stop it! Now you're embellishing. I never told you my arms were flailing."

"Shhh!" Zoey chastised as she hung on Brad's every word, her eyes big with unbridled glee.

"Nothing she tries stops her. Then, bam!" Brad cried, slapping his hands together for effect. "She goes plowing face first right into the window. I get there twenty minutes later, and I think some pervert's had their jollies on her window, but it's just where she went face first into the thing. When I looked"—he broke down laughing—"when I looked, I could actually see the outline of her face. Distorted like a horror show, but it was her."

"There's something wrong with you," Joel said while Brad stood bent double with his hands on his knees, trying to catch his breath.

"I still don't understand how someone could call in a complaint against you for indecent exposure," Jack said. "It must have been whoever was outside your window. Weren't they concerned about getting caught?"

"It was an anonymous call," I said.

"They called using the old pay phone on the side of the old Wal-Mart," Brad said, finally regaining his composure. "Disguised their voice. Could have been anyone."

"Sweetheart," Agatha said, "did you get a look at whoever was outside your window?"

"Nooo, they cut through my string of sparkly lights. Ruined them, and everything was in shadow."

"This is the third time someone has tried to break into your place by way of the fire escape," Joel said. He hadn't been laughing at all, and he didn't look happy that Brad had. "It needs a security system, and I'm going to help you set one up."

"I can't afford one," I hurriedly said, then felt my cheeks heat at the admission. The truth was that the fairy lights I'd put outside had been a hard stretch for my budget. Now they were gone.

"Naw, I've got it covered. I've got a wedge tapped into the hinge side of that weird window-door of hers. Only way that window is going to open is if that wedge is removed, and a person would need to be already inside to do that. If someone is outside and wants in, they'll have to break the glass, and it's some thick glass. Good quality. They'd have to work at it."

I headed into the kitchen. Brenda was walking me through making a big pot of chili. It wasn't my cousin Sarah's secret chili recipe, but Brenda figured she could get us close enough. It was already smelling good enough to go on the regular menu board instead of the Oops Board.

Zoey followed me back. "Indecent exposure?" she said.

"Yeah, I know. That's Tina's trick. She did it with Mike. And I didn't tell Brad this, but I spotted a small tin of lighter fluid on the ground beneath the fire escape. I think she dropped it when I startled her."

"She was meaning to set your apartment on fire," Zoey said. "We've got out killer."

"Now we've got to find a way to prove it."

CHAPTER 26

A morning of scrambled eggs, bacon and biscuits had moved seamlessly into an afternoon of chili and baked potatoes. Nothing but the first batch of biscuits had gone on the Oops Board.

Now I was sitting in Zoey's car across the street from Tina's house. Waiting and watching. Watching and waiting. Zoey was getting impatient.

"We could burn her out. Do to her what she'd planned to do to you."

A part of me liked that idea. A lot. But a bigger part of me didn't want to go to prison for arson. "Maybe she's taking a nap." We'd walked around her whole house, peeking in the windows. We hadn't been able to see anything, though. Turns out that someone obsessed with watching others is especially guarded about others watching them. From all the effort we'd put into trying to get a glimpse of the inside of her house, beyond what we'd already seen of her foyer, I couldn't even say if she had carpet or hardwood floors.

"Maybe we could—"

A tap on my passenger side window cut Zoey off and made us both jump. Turning my head with the expectation of seeing Tina's bug eyes staring back at me, I breathed a sigh of relief when I instead saw a handsome, well-groomed man in his late 40s to early 50s. He was tethered to a dog or a dog was tethered to him—I couldn't tell which. One of them was taking the other one for a walk, and since the dog looked as though it weighed my and Zoey's weight combined, I thought it was a toss-up as to which one of them was in charge.

I power rolled my window down.

"Hi," the man said, all smiles. The dog didn't smile, but I did see some teeth. "I'm Gerald Thompson. You're parked in front of my house." He motioned to the house behind him. "Is there something I can do for you?"

"Sorry about that," I said. "We were hoping to talk to Tina."

The big shaggy dog leaned against his leash, and Gerald's arm was pulled out to full extension, but he held his spot next to the car. "Tina teaches a gymnastics class on Monday afternoon. She won't be back for a while yet."

I looked at Zoey. Monday afternoon. Mike had died last Monday. If Tina taught a class on Mondays, she wouldn't have been here to do it.

"Do you know what time she usually leaves on Mondays to go to her class?" Zoey asked.

"I come home for lunch and to walk Button most days," Gerald said.

I couldn't help myself. I had to interject. I glanced over at the dog. If he sneezed, he could swallow Sage whole on the inhale. "You named him Button?"

"It was my wife's doing. When we brought him home, she'd said he was cute as a button. It stuck."

"You were saying," Zoey said, getting us back on track.

"Tina usually leaves for class at the same time I head back to work, around twelve forty-five."

Mike was already dead and cooling by that time last Monday. That meant that Tina could still have done it.

"What time did you get home for lunch last Monday?" I asked.

"Usual time, around eleven-thirty."

"And Tina was here?"

He shrugged. "Don't know. She keeps her car in her garage. Well, and there was such a commotion that day with the ambulance and the police cars. I don't recall seeing her." Out of the corner of my eye I saw a squirrel dart across the road in front of Zoey's car. Button saw it too. He lunged, but like a trooper, Button's owner dug his heels in and held onto Zoey's car's side mirror. His voice now strained from his battle of wills with Button, he asked, "You're not thinking that Tina had anything to do with Mike's death, are you?"

I put the question back on him. "Do you think she could have had anything to do with his death?" Button lunged again. Gerald's footing slipped, and his whole torso slammed against the car. He found new leverage, though, by looping his hand through the open window and holding onto the frame of the car while he continued the conversation through the front windshield. "She's a character, but she's a good neighbor. Keeps a beautiful yard. I'm sure she had nothing to do with it."

I saw Zoey's hand move for the windshield wiper control and slapped her hand away.

The dog lunged again, once more body slamming Gerald against the car.

"Do you need any help?" I asked. I was growing concerned. One more good jerk from Button, and I was sure that his arm was going to be ripped right off.

"Do you recall anyone else here the morning that Mike died?" Zoey asked, not giving Gerald a chance to answer if he needed help. Button lunged again and this time Gerald lost his hold on the car and was pulled spread-eagle onto the hood of the car. I put my hands over my mouth to keep from yelping with concern, but Zoey yelled, "Anyone at all?"

Gerald answered a garbled "Nooo!" or "Awww!" before he disappeared off the front of the car. I wasn't sure which.

Zoey turned to me. "I call that inconclusive."

She started the car, put it in reverse, and maneuvered away. The last I saw of Gerald was of him being dragged across the road in short lurches of two or three feet at a time.

"Where to next?" Zoey asked once we'd gotten out of view of Gerald.

I said the first name that came to mind. "Betty. Let's go talk to Betty."

The drive took fifteen minutes, and I kept replaying Tina's words in my head.

"What?" Zoey asked, prompting me to share what was on my mind.

"When we talked to Tina, she said that she'd seen those two beauticians over at Mike's."

"Two of 'em? What, you thinking Susie *and* Betty?"

"Yeah."

"I didn't think Betty rented from Mike," Zoey said.

"I hadn't either. I mean, I think she *wanted* us to make that assumption, but I don't recall her actually ever saying that she didn't rent from Mike."

"Why would she do that?"

"Don't know. Pride?" I remembered times when Dan and I had attended swanky parties alongside powerful business moguls. Without outright lying about it, Dan would phrase things in such a way as to make it sound like our—his—company had been doing two or three times better than it actually was.

"Could be. We already know that she'd

been spreading nasty rumors about Susie's abilities. She'd been doing everything she could to scare Susie's clients off and steal them for herself."

"Yeah... So I guess that tells us that not everything that comes out of her mouth is trustworthy."

"But Tina said something about someone else, too. She mentioned someone who she specifically said did not rent from Mike. Gina... Janice..."

"Grace!" I said, snapping my fingers.

"Yeah, Grace," Zoey said as she parked in front of Betty's salon, *Betty's Beauties*. "So, if Grace didn't have business with Mike..."

"Then that meant she was visiting Mike for personal reasons," I said.

"Bingo."

We got out of the car. I could see Betty working inside her salon. She could practically see the whole other side of the street from inside her shop. It was the perfect vantage point.

I turned around and looked at the shops on the other side of the street, wondering if they had as good a view of Betty's place as she had of theirs. I'd have to walk that side of the street and even pop inside the various businesses, but I already knew that most of the shops didn't look out through a huge wall of glass the way that Betty's did. Her vantage point was better than anyone else's to keep tabs on the rest of the world.

Betty's door jingled from an overhead bell when we pushed inside. Betty was with a client, and I had to walk several feet into the shop and lean to the side before I could tell whether or not her other two hairdressers were there with her. They weren't.

"Well, what are you two sweethearts doin' back here?" Betty asked as she pinned a curl in place at the nape of her client's neck. As before, she was the consummate southern beauty queen with a warm welcoming smile and an approachable friendliness that made me genuinely want to grab a seat, put my feet up and flip casually through some magazines. Something about her made me forget the troubles of the rest of the world. "You gonna finally let me give you a trim? Julia here is gonna be going under the blower in just a few minutes and I can fit you in then."

Wanting to keep things as casual as possible, rather than giving an air of confrontation, I took a seat in front of one of the low coffee tables, and Zoey sat down next to me. "Betty, do you own your shop?"

"Well of course I do, honey. It's got my name on it."

The gears in my head turned and strained. I was sure that Betty was playing with words, a flawless misdirection on her part. She owned her business, but I was asking if she owned the physical location of her shop. "So you own this building?"

"Oh goodness, no," Betty said laughing. "That would lock me into this location. It's much better to be able to relocate to the most advantageous and popular shopping spots. Foot traffic. You simply cannot beat the free advertising that being in a high foot traffic area will give you. I'm sure you know that with your prime spot there on Main Street, though." She gave me a wink. "Can you tell a difference in your clientele flow during the hours with the highest foot traffic?"

I'd give her foot traffic—my sneaker right into her mouth. She was so likable, so easy to talk to, that I wanted to answer her question, but another part of me had figured her out. She was trying to guide the conversation to what she wanted to talk about... and away from what she didn't want to talk about.

Ignoring her question, I asked, "Who owns this building?"

Betty's eyes got wide and she asked in a conspiratorial tone, "Kylie Berry, are you thinking of adding to your property holdings? Are you thinking of snapping up Mike's old properties?"

Again, she was directing the conversation. It was so hard for me to keep a steady hand on the proverbial rudder and to keep moving forward in the direction I wanted to go. "So Mike did own this property?"

"Well of course he did, silly," Betty said with a Tinkerbell laugh. "He owned just about everything on this street."

The way she said it made me feel as though it had been my fault for not knowing the truth from the very beginning. Betty was not only directing the conversation, but she was trying to direct my perceptions as well. The woman was good.

"And you paid him rent?" Zoey asked.

"Same as everyone else, darlin'," Betty answered, but now her voice had gained an edge. "What's this about?"

"Where are your two other hairdressers?" Zoey asked.

"At a conference showcasing new hair care products in Cincinnati. Want me to give you their phone numbers?" Sarcasm dripped from her tone. "Now, I am with a client, so that is the end of your questions—"

It was my turn to press. "You were here all day last Monday?"

Betty stopped fussing with her client's hair, turned to face us, and threw her hands out wide in exasperation. "Ugh. Still trying to save your precious Susie? The woman's a killer, plain and simple. Accept it and move on!" She pointed at a small, simple, all white desk-top table on the other side of the shop. "There. There," she said, wagging her finger. "There's my appointment book. We—all three of us—had appointments all day long last Monday. You don't believe me? Look for yourself." With another exasperated sound, she turned her back on us and put her hands on her client's shoulders. "Julia, I am sooo sorry. I am alll yours. Let's get you beautiful."

It was clear that Betty was cutting us off without another word. Without saying anything, Zoey and I went to her appointment book and flipped it back to the previous Monday, the day that Mike had died. As promised, it listed non-stop appointments from as early as eight AM that morning to after six that evening. It was a lot of information to take in, and I pulled out my phone and took a couple of pictures of it to look through more closely later.

Back outside on the sidewalk, I turned to Zoey. “Did you see that? Did you see how she tried to talk around what we wanted to know?”

“I did, but I hope she didn’t do it.”

“Why?”

“I really liked those finger sandwiches she gave us last time. Think if we got back in and make nice that she’ll give us some more?”

I scowled in answer.

“No, huh? Okay, let’s go hit up some of the shops up the street. Maybe they saw something.”

CHAPTER 27

"What is this place?" I asked as Zoey parked in a nearly deserted parking lot, one big enough to accommodate the needs of a super-sized Walmart. There wasn't another car around for a hundred feet in any direction.

"It's the gift shop," Zoey said.

"*This* is the *gift shop?*" There was no way. The building attached to the parking lot looked like a contemporary re-imagining of a castle. It was huge and even had tall, spear-like spires. "What's it made out of? Is that a stone façade?" The building's stone bricks were enormous. They were fe-fi-fo-fum giant sized stone bricks. I'd seen buildings in Chicago made out of stone bricks far less impressive, buildings I hadn't been allowed inside of because I was nowhere near posh enough to make it past the doorman.

"Nope, they're real."

I shook my head in disbelief. "How... just how?"

"Come on," Zoey said, getting out of the car.

Huge, arched, bronze letters spelled out "Camden Falls Artisan Center" across the building's front. We'd come here to find Grace after the shops up the street from Betty's salon had been a bust for information. Well, that wasn't completely true. The shops had been full of people with plenty to say about Mike's murder, or rather who they thought had committed the murder. At the convenience store, wagers were being placed on how much prison time Susie would have to do. And at the nail salon—where they either didn't speak English or pretended not to speak English—Susie's name was thrown around accompanied by gales of laughter.

The one thing we had learned was that everybody on Brunt Street, with the exception of Betty who believed that Tina had done it, thought that Susie was guilty of murdering Mike Pratt. Nobody had any information that pointed to the contrary, and worse yet, nobody had been interested in considering any other possibility.

Things were not looking good for Susie.

"How is this even possible?" I said, still in awe of what the sleepy little town of Camden Falls called a "gift shop." I walked slowly next to Zoey, taking my time to drink in all the sights. The building was fronted by a very deep and curving outer courtyard. Placed throughout were a myriad of human-sized steel sculptures. There was a horse riding a Harley, a big whiskered cat was using a mouse as a yo-yo, and an old hound dog playing a banjo. The craftsmanship was undeniable, and the laminated price tags were downright scary.

"I dunno," Zoey said with a shrug. "This place was here before I got here." That wasn't saying much. Zoey had only lived in Camden Falls for about a year. "Everything in it was made by Kentucky artists. That's all I know."

"Unbelievable." I had to reach for the building's door handle three times while I stared at a sculpture of a family of ladybugs traveling across the arched, steel rendering of a log. The mommy and daddy ladybugs had hobo knapsacks on sticks over their shoulders, and each of their little ones carried smaller ones too.

With my eyes still on the sculpture, taking in every detail I could, I barreled straight into a wall of chest and bounced backward.

"I'm sorry!" I said, the words out of my mouth before my eyes had a chance to see who I was saying them to. When I did see, the only thing more out of me was a squeak—that is until Zoey ran into the back of me and sent me bouncing off that wall of man chest all over again.

I released a choked screech and jumped back so hard and so fast that the man in front of me might as well have been on fire.

"What gives?" Zoey asked, annoyance and concern laced into her voice in equal measures.

I coughed and then cleared my throat before trying to speak. "This is, uh, this is Dan," I said.

Zoey looked him up and down. "Want me to hurt him? I could run him over with my car."

It was a tempting offer, but there was too much risk of our attempt at vehicular homicide being witnessed by some innocent bystander—"Dan? Dan where are you?" my ex-aunt Dorothy's voice called from a distance—or by some not-so-innocent bystander.

"Any chance you could get two for one?" I asked Zoey under my breath.

Zoey shrugged. "There's always a first time."

That made me wonder and worry that maybe there had been a time that she'd done a one-for-one vehicular homicide. It registered as yet another note-to-self to never get on Zoey's bad side.

"Always with the murdering," Dan crooned. "What is it with my exes? First you and now Susie."

I narrowed my eyes and squeezed my nails into the palms of my hands. "I was found innocent and Susie will be too, but I'm sure that one of your three-thousand or so other conquests won't fail to disappoint."

Dan seemed charmed rather than off-put by my flaring temper.

"Kylie, sweetheart, how have you been?" He leaned in to kiss my cheek, and like a dullard who was thinking too slowly, I didn't pull away in time. His scratchy cheek brushed mine, I caught a whiff of his scent and—despite everything I'd been through and all that I knew about him—he made my toes curl. "You look *amazing*," he said into my ear, and darn it all but I leaned into him. It was only Zoey's hand on the back of my neck that tore me from his spell. Dan and I had our issues, but our time together in the bedroom had never been one of them. I supposed that had something to do with the things he'd learned during his many, many, many forays into extracurricular activity… with other women. Forays I most definitely had been kept in the dark about.

As to his "amazing" comment, I was wearing my red princess-style coat and a plain white V-neck t- over top of the jeans I used to wear when cleaning our one-time home. Yet his compliment sounded sincere. We'd been together for eight and a half years. I'd known him well enough to know when he was lying, and at least as far as he was concerned, he wasn't lying.

I decided to accept that flattery, but not the man doling it out—even if he did look like a quarterback who had never left his prime.

"What are you doing here?" I asked.

"I grew up here. You knew that when

you moved here from Chicago. Don't act like you didn't have hopes of seeing me again." His hand ran down the length of my arm. "I'm just glad I didn't disappoint."

I opened my mouth to say something —something cutting, something mean, something that would make it unnecessary for him to ever have a vasectomy— but my ex-aunt Dorothy's voice calling him in the background stole all my thoughts.

Dan looked over his shoulder and then back at me. His smugness dropped away, leaving me unnerved to be looking up at the man I'd fallen in love with all those years ago. He gave me a wink. "I've got'cha. You go that way." He side-nodded toward the set of doors on the opposite end of the wide entryway and then turned his back on us and threw his arms wide. In a booming voice that I was sure could have been heard by half the absurdly large "gift shop," he said, "Aunt Dorothy! Where have you been all my life?"

Taking full advantage of Dan's diversion, Zoey and I zipped to the far door and dashed through. Ex-aunt Dorothy's eyes were disturbingly only for Dan as she made her way to him, but that left Zoey and me in the free and clear as Dan and his aunt left the building, a shopping bag dangling from her arm.

"So that's Dan?" Zoey said, her eyes twinkling. "He's different than in his pictures online. I get it now."

I slapped her arm. "You get nothing." I knew she was teasing, but her words held truth. Dan was charisma incarnate. It was part of why he'd been able to keep me dazzled so long by all the parts he'd wanted me to see and blinded to all the parts of himself he hadn't wanted me to see. "Let's find Grace."

Zoey and I wandered our way through the large, sprawling building. We drifted from section to section. It even had a café on one end. Thankfully, the whole place had an open floor plan and that made spotting the center's employees relatively fast and easy work. They were all dressed in khakis and lime green shirts with name tags. It didn't take long to spot Grace. She was tall, slender, and like so many others of Mike's conquests, she had thick black hair. Hers fell in long layers down her back. She looked to be in her mid-twenties and was pretty enough to be a personality on a local morning talk show on TV.

Zoey and I watched her answer questions about a set of handcrafted lutes and then swooped in as soon as the curious customer headed on their way. But I wasn't prepared for what I saw when we got up close. Grace's makeup was flawless, but peeking through from underneath were dark circles under her eyes and a slight tremor in her hands. She didn't look tired. She looked exhausted.

I don't know what I had planned to ask her, but everything changed when I saw her up close. "Can we buy you a cup of tea or coffee in the café?" Grace's eyes glanced around us, I assumed in search of her boss. I touched her hand to refocus her on me. "If anyone asks, I'll tell them that I needed to be able to sit because of sciatica and that we asked you to sit with us so that we could learn more about the center."

That seemed to do the trick, and even earned us a faint smile and a small nod.

While Zoey and Grace got us seats at a table overlooking a large pond with a water spouting fountain at its center, I got coffee and chocolate chocolate-chip muffins for everyone. I was afraid that Zoey would be in the process of disemboweling Grace for information by the time I reached the table, but, in rare form, Zoey was sitting quietly and she and Grace were looking out over the pond, watching the spray from the spouting fountain dance across the water's surface.

Sitting down at a table where no one was talking felt more odd than sitting down at a table mid-conversation. It was awkward. The silence felt pregnant. Finally, Grace pulled her attention away from the pond and looked at me.

"You're trying to figure out who killed Mike, aren't you?" she said.

Zoey and I looked at each other.

"I know about you two. Heard about you. My brother went to school with that guy who everybody said you killed," she said, looking at Zoey. "He said you two figured out the truth." Then she looked at me. "And my mom goes to church with your Aunt Dorothy."

"Ex-aunt," I said, the words coming out of my mouth all on their own.

"I've heard so much about you."

"None of it's true. I swear," I said. My ex-aunt Dorothy hated me. When I first took over the café, she told everyone that I'd kill people with my food. Then, of course, somebody ate my food and died. So, yeah, they weren't good times.

"I was hoping that it was all true." She leaned forward onto her elbows. The exhaustion I saw in her eyes made me want to make up a pallet on the floor right then and there and watch over it as she took a nap. "Somebody killed Mike. They stole years away from his life, and I want to know who it was."

"How long was Mike your boyfriend?"

I asked. I had no idea if he was, but Grace was the first person we'd met who seemed to have been affected by his death.

"A few years."

Bingo! Except Mike was a horndog. He tried to extort women for sex. If they were nice to him, he'd be nice about their rent. It was the type of information that could totally shut down this conversation...

"We had an open relationship."

Or maybe not.

"And before you ask, I was here all day the day Mike died. All day. You can ask my boss. You can ask anyone I work with. I didn't kill Mike, but I want to know who did."

Grace was a beautiful woman full of youth. Mike had been an out of shape old geezer by comparison—an old geezer whom she knew slept with whatever skirt he could catch.

"If you don't mind me asking," I said, "why were you with Mike?"

"Money."

Her face didn't flinch. I didn't even see any shame.

She shrugged. "I like nice things. He could give me nice things. He liked pretty women. I'm a pretty woman. We knew who we were to each other and we were fine with it. We were more than fine with it. We were happy. We saw each other when we wanted to see each other. I never put any pressure on him about who we were to each other, never asked for a commitment, and he never tried to tell me how to live my life. All those other idiot women, I'd hear about how they'd try to play him, how they'd try to manipulate him. They always wanted. Always tried to trick him, so he got off on tricking them instead."

I was a bit surprised at the words that were coming out of her mouth. So young, but so jaded. I'd never been a huge sisterhood solidarity type of person, putting women before any man ever, but I did feel compassion for the many women who had been messed over by a man in some way or other.

Zoey shifted in her chair. "Did any of the women he tricked want to hurt Mike?"

"All of them," Grace scoffed. "But none of them had a use for Mike six feet in the ground. They all wanted what he could do for them while he was alive. So I don't get it. I don't get why one of them would kill him."

"But you're convinced that it was a woman?" I asked.

She nodded.

"Why?"

She shrugged. "No blood. Guys, they want to know they've been there. They want to leave a mark. Whoever killed Mike, they let that stupid machine of his do all the work."

That made sense. When I thought of murder by men, I did tend to picture an end that required a blood splatter analysis afterward. Women didn't seem as interested in making a mess.

I leaned onto my elbows, mirroring Grace. "Who do you think did it?"

"Well, not Susie," Grace said with open

derision. "I've talked to the police five different times now. Five. They haven't told me who they think did it, haven't named names, but every question they ask tracks back to Susie. They're building a case instead of solving it."

Holy cow. Someone who knew Mike and didn't think that Susie had killed him.

"Why don't you think it was Susie?" I asked, feeling way too eager for her answer.

"She's too much of a wimp."

Not a flattering answer, but it at least it was an argument toward Susie's defense.

Zoey sat back and crossed her arms. "Yeah, I'm not buying it. Wimps explode when pushed too far. Calling Susie a wimp doesn't prove anything."

I felt like kicking Zoey under the table. We'd finally found someone willing to entertain the idea that Susie was innocent. But Zoey had a point. The defense of "she's a wimp" wasn't going to stand up in any court of law.

"You got anything else?" I asked

Grace. "Anything you could tell us about the other women in Mike's life?"

"Betty wanted to marry him and—"

"Wait. What? She what?" I asked, thankful that I was already sitting down.

"Yeah. Mike would laugh about it. He'd talk about how she'd drop hints left and right about him needing to buy her an engagement ring. She was picking out places for them to go on a honeymoon, and she'd ask questions about people like she was putting together a guest list. She was nuts—but he thought it was cute."

My stomach turned upside down. Mike had thought Betty wanting to marry him was "cute."

"How long had this cuteness been going on?" Zoey asked.

Grace shrugged. "Six, seven months?"

My head was spinning, but Grace was such a well of information. I had to hold it together. "Had he done anything to make her think that they would be getting married?"

Grace shrugged again. "I don't know. Maybe. She was so eager. She doted on him. Baked for him, cleaned his house, did anything he asked. He liked it… but he was going to end it."

"Why?" I asked.

"She got possessive. Started wanting him to account for his time. Started making demands. It became not fun for him anymore, so he was going to end it."

Not fun… I hoped that Mike was rotting in his grave.

"Was he seeing any other women while he and Betty were a couple?" Zoey asked.

"Other than me? Sure. Lots. Sometimes they were just flings for a weekend. Sometimes a couple of weeks. I think that the only reason he stayed with Betty so long was that she was a great cook. She'd make homemade meals for him. Brought a girl's touch to his house. He said she made it feel more like a home. But… she was kind of like a vacation for him. I knew it would never last."

"Do you know if he'd broken up with Betty already before the time of his death?" I asked.

"I don't think so."

"Do you think that Betty killed him?"

"No, I think it was Clara."

Yes! My ego led an instant and silent little cheer, and I realized that I needed to do a lot of self-checking later about my jealousy over her success with her coffee shop.

"Why Clara?" Zoey asked.

"Mike had been trying to get her into bed for forever, but she'd been smart about it. She wanted a new contract, one that locked in her rent rates for half of what she was paying. He told me that he'd finally had a contract drawn up but that he'd had a clause built into it that would nullify and void the contract even after it had been signed. He planned to sleep with her and then legally revert back to the original contract."

"Do you know if he'd gone through with it by the time of his death?"

"I think so. He didn't say so directly, but I know that he'd planned to do it soon. So I think he slept with her, then told her that the new contract was worthless, and she killed him."

That would make me want to kill him.

"What about loony-toons next door?" Zoey asked.

"Tina? Yeah, she's psycho."

"But you don't think it was her?" I asked.

"Tina and Mike had a thing several years back, before my time. She'd been all up in his stuff ever since I'd known him. Unhinged. Crazy. Obsessive. She is not right in the head. But that's the way it's always been. She's always been like that. What could have made her go from being the crazy psycho lady to being the crazy killer lady after all that time? And there wasn't anything in it for her to kill Mike."

"How do you mean?" I asked.

"If she killed Mike, who would she have to obsess over and throw all her hate at?"

Grace had a point.

Zoey tapped the table top with one nail-bitten finger. "What if Betty got even more ahead of herself and let slip to Tina that she and Mike were going to get married?"

"Ohhhh," Grace said. "Ohhhh, yeah. Tina's head would have exploded at the thought of Mike having a happily ever after. If she thought that Mike was in love and happy..." She shook her head. "I don't think that Tina could have lived with that. Her whole purpose in life was trying to create misery in his."

I couldn't imagine letting hate so fully consume everything good about my life. "Why'd she hate him so much?"

Grace shook her head. "I don't know. I don't think Mike knew. I think their fling only lasted a month and a half. But... they had been flirting for close to a year. He'd said that there'd been a lot of build up before they got into it. Then they got into it and things were off the hook intense, but by the time they came up for air, he'd gotten all he wanted. Dropped her cold turkey."

"And this happened...?"

"A few years back. Not recent," Grace said.

"So," Zoey said, "Tina gets her jollies hating on Mike. Betty tells Tina that she and Mike are heading for a happily ever after. That sends Tina off the deep end, and she kills Mike."

"That's what happened, it's got to be," Grace said. "Tina killed Mike."

But that left some seriously unanswered questions about Clara…

CHAPTER 28

"What's the plan?" I asked. We were back in our spot across the road from Tina's house. The light outside was failing, and I was worried about whether or not the chili and baked potatoes prepared for lunch would last to cover all of the dinner customers, however few there would be.

"We go up and knock on Tina's door. If she answers, we press her until she confesses to Mike's murder. If she doesn't answer, we find a way in and search her house."

"For what? Mike was killed with his own shredder and his own scarf. What evidence could she have stashed away?"

"I don't know. Maybe she's got one of those love-you-to-death shrines in her house."

"A what shrine?"

"You know, some closet or room where she's pasted pictures of him all over her wall and scratched out his eyes and stuff like that."

"Eww, that's sick," I said, picturing all the imaginary carnage.

"Of course it's sick. Look who we're talking about."

"Shut. The. Front. Door."

"Yeah, we'll shut the front."

"No, no… Look! Tina's shutting the front door!" Zoey snapped her head around to look at Tina's front door. "No! Mike's front door! Tina's coming out of Mike's house!"

As we watched, Tina balanced a load of items in her arms while picking up a rock, doing something to the bottom of it. She then tossed it into the bushes to the side of the door.

"A hide-a-key rock," Zoey said.

We watched Tina look up and down

the street before cutting across Mike's yard toward her own.

Zoey and I got out of her car, and Tina spotted us when I closed my car door too hard. She froze, then she ran. Zoey and I burst into a hard sprint. All three of us were aiming for Tina's front door.

Tina jumped the low hedges separating her yard from Mike's. Zoey and I burst through a line of young rose bushes. Tina reached her door first, but then fumbled trying to get it open because of all the stuff in her arms. It slowed her down just enough for Zoey to pull Tina back by the collar of her shirt before wedging herself in-between Tina and the front door.

I was very embarrassingly huffing by the time I reached the door. Zoey and Tina weren't winded at all. I really needed to start fitting in some cardio into my day.

Zoey shot the first question at Tina. "Why'd you try to break into Kylie's apartment?"

"No, I didn't. Why would I?" Tina was more wild-eyed than usual. It made me concerned that we didn't have something like a netted fish scoop on hand to pick them up if they popped out of her head.

"What were you doing in Mike's house?" I said.

"I wasn't in his house. I was just coming home. I just got here."

The lie was so blatant. It was an attempt to completely rewrite history. Too bad her car was nowhere in sight.

"Isn't your car parked in your garage?" I asked. "Don't you have a door leading from your garage into your house? Why would you be out in your yard, going through your front door with a… a"—I took a quick inventory of the items in her arms—"stapler? And what is that, a man's hairbrush? What about that shaving kit?"

"Shut up. You don't know what you're talking about. I just got home."

"Tina!" I knew that it was her word against ours, but we did at least have some physical evidence on our side that I was sure could be IDed as belonging to

Mike if we tried hard enough. "We saw you come out of Mike's house. Zoey's got video of it on her phone!" It was an outright lie, but it would hopefully move us past Tina's outright lie.

Tina looked back and forth between me and Zoey. She looked like she was watching a tennis match played at hyper speed, then the unthinkable happened. Her huge bulging eyes squeezed shut and she burst out into tears. "I just wanted a memento," she sobbed. "He was mine. I loved him. Nobody understood us. Nobody understood what we had. I just wanted something of his that I could hold onto."

I looked at what she'd chosen again. I could understand the hairbrush and the shaving kit. Those two were very personal items, but the stapler did fit in. It was a stapler. Completely non-personal. Meaningless.

"You killed him with the stapler, did you?" I blurted.

"No. What are you saying? He choked."

"But he could have gotten away, couldn't he? He could have gotten himself loose. But you were there, and you hit him on the back of his head with *that* stapler, didn't you!"

"No!"

"Admit it! You found out that he and Betty were getting married—"

"What?!" Tina's screech was so loud and so shrill that I was shocked that I wasn't hearing the sound of glass break all up and down the street.

Tina's cradling arms dropped their precious cargo and her stolen items fell to the concrete stoop with a clatter. Then she pushed me. Hard. I'd been completely unprepared for her reaction, and I ended up flat on my back several feet away.

I was also not prepared for what happened after that. Tina screamed "Take it back!" and then leaped through the air like Spiderman to land straddling my chest with her knees pinning down my arms.

"Take it back!" she screamed again as her hands clamped themselves around my neck with the strength of a steel vice. I thrashed beneath her, but I couldn't get my arms loose to defend myself at all.

Zoey looped an arm around Tina's waist and lifted her off. Even then, Tina kept her hold on my neck. With me prying her hands loose and Zoey pulling her, I finally broke free and Zoey flung Tina into the middle of her yard.

Tina turned the momentum into a gymnast's tumble and landed in complete control of her body. On all fours, in a position poised to launch her forward in another attack, she screamed, "Take it back! He was mine! He was coming back to me!"

Zoey and I inched ourselves closer together. Strength in numbers.

"Just a guess," I said, "but I think that this might be the first time she's hearing about any wedding plans."

"I agree. She would have definitely left blood splatter."

I imagined Tina hitting Mike with the stapler. Then I imagined her hitting him a few hundred more times with the stapler.

Yep, definitely blood splatter.

"Race you to the car?" I asked.

"No, walk with arms linked. She'll want to separate us to take us down one at a time. Rip our throats out or something."

The day had almost fully turned into night, but I was pretty sure that I could see some foamy spittle on Tina's mouth. Deranged didn't even begin to describe her at that moment.

"Yep," I said. "Strength in numbers. Let's do this."

CHAPTER 29

Making it back to Zoey's car had been like trying to maneuver past a rabid dog. Don't move too fast, don't move too slow. We locked the doors the second we got inside, and Zoey was driving as soon as the car slipped into gear.

"Where to next?" Zoey asked once Tina was out of sight. "Betty's salon?"

"The café. I've got to get back," I said, looking at my phone with still shaking hands. I'd gotten a text from Melanie. "The chili's almost gone, and they don't have anything to serve for dinner."

Zoey parked behind the café so that I

could get inside and get to work that much quicker. I entered through the back into the kitchen, grabbed an apron, threw it on, and then went out to the Oops Board. I'd made enough steak hoagies as practice. Now it was time to offer an actual steak dinner. I scrawled the menu onto the board: sirloin, steak fries, caramelized onions, and grilled plum tomatoes with blue cheese crumble. I was going bold.

"Kylie?" Melanie's voice called from nearby behind me.

"Yes?" I said, putting a final swirl on the board before giving her my attention.

"You have a visitor." Melanie pointed over her shoulder, and that's when I spotted her. Winnie. She was one of the homeless people who had stayed the night in the café.

"The cookies!" I hissed, exhilaration flooding me. All the sudden, the café's future didn't feel so bleak and fragile. It felt robust and certain. With Winnie's cookies baking in my kitchen, I'd have more business than I knew what to do with.

Winnie looked tired and a little ragged, but she was here. I could work with that. Things had a chance of getting better for both of us.

Leaving the finished menu behind, I went to the wall-side table where Winnie sat. Even though it was at night, the blind was pulled on the window next to her, blocking the view out to the street.

"Hi," I said. "Do you mind if I sit?"

Winnie's face brightened when she looked up and saw me, but her eyes retained a haunted look. Then when her gaze darted around us, I realized that I'd read her wrong. She was hunted, not haunted. She was still wearing her coat, and she had a bag gripped tightly in her lap. She was ready to run at an instant's notice.

Winnie nodded for me to sit, and I pulled out the chair across from her.

"What's wrong, Winnie?" It was hard for me not to ask about the cookies before anything else, but there were things more important in life than those cookies or even my café. She had look life-worn when I'd first met her, but now she looked downright haggard. The creases on her face seemed somehow deeper and harsher, as if they'd been carved there rather than developed over time.

"I, uh, need your help. I need some money."

Oh no… I could feed her. I could even give her shelter. And, I'd love to be able to give her a job. But money… I was in short supply of that myself. "Winnie, it's just that—"

"Jackson is trying to kill me," Winnie blurted before I could give her the bad news. "I was supposed to sell some pills for him, but Derek stole them. I don't take 'em. None of 'em. Not me. I'm clean. But Derek gets real sick if he don't take somethin', and he found the bag I had for Jackson and he took it. I know he did. He was sufferin' and then he started being fine. He's got them, but I don't want to tell Jackson. He'll kill Derek, and he'll say I owe him for what Derek used up. And if I don't tell him what Derek done, then he'll say I stole them all and he'll kill me. But if I leave town…"

My mind was whirling from Winnie's tale, but I was finally able to grasp and hold onto that last bit. She needed money to get out of town. Her life and Derek's life depended on it.

"So if I give you money, you'll use it for…?" I asked, letting my voice trail off.

"A bus ticket."

"A bus ticket," I repeated. But I imagined giving her money and that money being used to put something up her arm or nose instead. I studied her eyes. Her pupils didn't look like pinpricks, they didn't look like saucers, and they didn't have a shiny, wet ice look. What I did see was desperation and hope. Winnie needed this, and she was scared. "Give me a second," I said.

First thing I did was go into the kitchen. I wanted to help Winnie, and something she would need was something to eat. It needed to be something simple and something that would travel well. “Peanut butter and jelly,” I said. I got out all the stuff and made her three peanut butter and jelly sandwiches.

I then went to the cash register and took a look at its contents. It had been an okay day. There was enough there to get her a bus ticket and for her to have a little bit extra in her pocket whenever she got to wherever she was going. Taking the money would mean that the café would be operating heavily in the red today. It meant that I might even struggle to be able to buy more supplies to keep the café operational later, but I could manage. I could feature potato soup and a couple of other low-cost dishes to make up the difference. I could learn how to make rice and figure out how to work with beans. I had options. Winnie was running out of those.

I emptied the till drawer into a bag. All of it. Even the coins. Then I headed back over to Winnie and sat down. I pushed the bag of food over. “These are peanut butter and jelly sandwiches." I pushed over the other bag. "And this is all the money that I have to give."

Winnie peeked inside the money bag, then her eyes squeezed hard shut and a tear fell as she lifted her face as if in a silent prayer. When she opened her eyes and looked at me again, she was wearing her first smile of the night. "This is enough to get me to my sister's," she said. "I can maybe start over."

I squeezed her hand. "Do you need help getting to the bus station?" I knew that Zoey would be willing to take her.

Winnie leaned so that she could see past the blinds and out into the night. "I think I do."

I patted her hand. "You sit tight, and I'll give somebody a yell to take you."

I left Winnie where she sat and headed back to the kitchen. I took out my phone with the intention of texting Zoey, but then hesitated. There was Brad's name. He could take Winnie to the bus station, and no one would try to jump them because he was a uniformed cop. But him being in uniform might draw attention to them, too. Also, would Brad be required to arrest Winnie? She wasn't exactly in this situation because she'd been following the straight and narrow.

Biting my lip, I decided to risk it. I called Brad.

"Calderos," Brad said by way of answering his phone.

"I need your help with something," I said. I knew that he'd know it was me from the caller ID.

"You at the café?"

"Yeah."

"Do I need backup?"

I hesitated. "I don't think so."

Brad growled, then hung up. He showed up six minutes later. I already had a bunch of potatoes cut for the steak fries, and I had the oven heating. I was running around the kitchen like a dervish, trying to get the ball rolling on dinner. I'd already had one order come in, and my stomach was in knots knowing that it would be close to forty-five minutes before I'd be able to send their meal out to them.

"I'm here. What do you need?" Brad asked, one hand at rest on top of his holstered gun. "You need to put some salt and oil on those potato wedges or they're going to oxidize. They're gonna turn brown on you."

"Oh! Right, thanks!" I set to work doing as he'd said. "Winnie's outside in the café. She's, um, in a spot of trouble. There's somebody who wants to hurt her, and she needs to get out of town. She needs go to the bus station. I know I could ask Zoey to take her—"

"No. I'll take her."

I stopped what I was doing and looked at him. "You won't arrest her?"

"I haven't heard anything that she needs arresting for yet. You got something to tell me that she needs arresting for?"

I held my breath.

"Okay then," he said. "Since I'm not hearing anything, I guess there's nothing to do but to escort her safely out of town."

A slow smile curved his lips. “I reckon Jackson will be mighty ticked off to lose one of his runners, but you can’t please everybody.”

I blew out my breath in relief and smiled back. “Thanks, Brad.”

I left food preparation behind and headed out to the café in front of Brad so that Winnie wouldn’t get spooked. “Winnie, I’ve found someone to take you to the bus station. Nobody will mess with you with this person there, okay?”

I guess I wasn’t selling it well and that my nerves were showing through, because Winnie didn’t look completely convinced. She looked past me, saw Brad, and then reset her gaze on me with the most awful look of betrayal.

“He’s going to help you get on that bus, Winnie,” I whispered. “If anybody sees you, no one will mess with you.”

The look of betrayal dropped away and was replaced by a glimmer of hope as Winnie looked past me once more. After what felt like forever, she gave a nod, and

I got out of their way and watched Brad and Winnie leave together.

I savored what was probably going to be my biggest good Samaritan moment of the year, that is until I heard my customer cough. They wanted their food. I rushed back to the kitchen and got back to work.

CHAPTER 30

"The cookies! I can't believe I didn't ask Winnie about the cookies!" I hit my head on the stainless steel counters in the kitchen.

"It'll be okay," Melanie consoled. "The dinner service went great! I even got bigger tips tonight! Everybody loved your food."

"Really?" I stood up and gave Melanie all my rapt attention. She was throwing me a lifeline. "Everybody really did like it?"

"They loved it!"

I'd been nervous about it, but after the fifth dinner plate went out, I took the dinner off the Oops Board and charged full price. I'd have to rethink my idea about going with cheaper meals to make a higher margin. The steaks had been expensive, but the tomatoes, potatoes and onions had all been on the inexpensive side. With those inexpensive items paired with the meat, I was able to make a decent profit. If I had more nights like tonight, the café was going to be okay.

"Need any help cleaning up?" Melanie asked.

"No, go ahead and bus the tables and then take off. You've been fabulous, Melanie. Thank you for everything."

Melanie was gone in a flash, no doubt eager to reclaim her life. As for me, I got to work fixing a small, fresh pan of steak fries and crumble-topped tomatoes. There were enough caramelized onions to do for two more meals, and that's all I'd need. While the fries and tomatoes cooked, I cleaned. I'd always been good at cleaning, but now I was a pro. No movement was wasted. No second was lost. By the time the fries and tomatoes were cooked, the industrial dishwasher was loaded and the counters were gleaming.

I sent Zoey a text. "Come over for a steak dinner and wine?"

My phone buzzed almost immediately. "You had me at wine. Be right there."

It was pushing midnight by the time Zoey arrived, and I had our steaks cooked and our plates in hand on my way to the table.

"Lock it behind you," I called over my shoulder as she pushed through the café's front door.

Zoey sat at the small table I'd prepared, and I poured us each a glass of red.

Zoey's brows were arched in what I took to be a mixture of disbelief and surprise. "This looks amazing. You did this?"

"Yep! It's all me." I sat down and we dug in.

Zoey made her first bite one that was stacked with onion, tomato and blue cheese, and then the perfect slice of steak.

"Oh my God," she said around a full mouth. The disbelief was gone and all that was left was surprise.

"I did good?"

"You did *great*!"

We ate, drank, and laughed. It was good to have a moment to enjoy with Zoey that didn't include worrying who was trying to kill us or wondering if one of us was going to be heading off to prison. But the laughter and the talking stopped when the rattle of the café's front door reached my ears.

"Expecting anyone?" Zoey whispered.

I shook my head no.

Together, Zoey and I slid out of our seats and then duck walked up the length of the café until we were able to see who our late night visitor was. It was Patty, and she was scowling at the uncooperative door something fierce.

Standing up, I rushed to the door, unlocked it and let Patty in. "Is everything all right?" I worried that I was going to be getting news that Derek had been found out and was now bleeding out somewhere in the street.

Patty wrung her hands nervously. She had a thick, short build, and baby fine straight hair that lay on her head like a cap. Thankfully, her cold appeared to be gone. "I heard what you did for Winnie. It was real nice of you."

My gut clenched. She was about to lay her own sob story on me and ask me for money. How would I be able to say no? How *could* I say no?

"I wanted to fix you up some more cookie dough as a thank you."

I gasped, and without even thinking about it, I threw my arms around Patty in a big hug. She went stiff as a board, and when I pulled away, her eyes were wild and her face had gone pale. "I'm sorry. I'm sorry," I reassured. "It's just that those cookies you left have helped me out so much! I've been looking all over the place for you. I didn't know which of you had made them."

Some of Patty's color returned, she smiled shyly. "I heard."

Zoey claimed a nearby chair and sat. "How'd you learn to bake like that, Patty?"

"I—I worked at this bakery in New York for years. We won all kinds of awards. We'd have people lined up all the way down the block for our cakes and pastries."

"What happened?" Zoey asked, and I was thankful that she'd been the one to ask it. I wondered too but felt embarrassed being so forward as to contrast what Patty's life had been before with what it was now. Homeless and on her own.

Patty started wringing her hands again. "I, uh, started hearing voices and not doin' so well. I had to go away for a while. When I got done, the bakery wanted me back. They did. But the voices told me not to. Hank, the owner, he's gone now, and the shop closed. It's all gone now." Patty's own voice trailed off to nothing as she spoke.

"Well, I'm glad you're here now," I said. I did my best not to let her see me tear up. "Would you be interested in coming to work for me by any chance?"

Patty took a step back. Her mouth was slack, and her entire visage was filled with fear.

"Or not!" I said hurriedly. "You don't have to work for me. Not at all. No pressure."

Patty's mouth closed and her gaze darted all around as she nodded her head, but I wasn't sure if she was nodding it because she agreed with what I'd said or if her head was wobbling from her nerves being so completely worn out. But then she took a deep breath, and it was like a new strength filled her. She smiled. "I'm going to make pecan sandies with a roasted marshmallow topping."

I'd never heard of such a thing, but I wasn't about to complain.

"And I'm going to make red velvet cake cookies, and ginger sugar cookies."

I desperately fought the urge to grab her in another big hug. "Patty," I said, knowing that I was about to test the boundaries of what she could handle, "do you think I could learn from you?"

"Oh… Oh." She looked me up and down like I might suddenly morph into the boogie man. "Um, yes?" Her eyes moved around her head like she was listening to something only she could hear. Then she smiled big, and said, "Yes."

"Ah! That's great!"

"But not tonight."

"Okay." It was my turn for my head to bob up and down in an out of control nod. "Whenever's good for you. Anytime. Day or night."

She smiled, patted my arm, and then trundled off to the kitchen. I did not follow her. If that woman was making me more cookies, there was no way that I was going to risk jinxing it by scaring her away. Instead I did a little happy dance and got a high five from Zoey before we returned to eating our dinner. It didn't take long for our conversation to get around to Mike and his murderer.

"Are you ready to cross Tina off our list of suspects?" I asked.

"No way. She's straight up nuts. She could have killed him and then blocked the whole thing out."

"Yeah, I didn't get the sense that she knew she'd done it—if she did do it."

"That leaves Susie—"

"I still don't think it was her."

"Betty—"

"Not sure what her motive would be if she didn't yet know that Mike was dumping her. Of course, it's super weird that she's not grieving his death."

"Super weird," Zoey agreed. "And there's also Clara."

Clara with her perfect coffee house. Prices higher than I'd dream of charging. Customers at every table. "I think it's her."

"Really?" Zoey said.

"What?"

"You hate her."

"I do not."

"You totally do. If her place got Molotoved, my first thought would be to find out if you needed an alibi."

"Ahhhh, you'd be my fake alibi?" I was so touched.

"You know it."

"Okay, so what do we do? Who do you think it was?" I asked.

"I say we go talk to Clara. I don't know if she did it, but I think that she could have done it."

"I think Betty might be covering for Clara or Clara might be covering for Betty."

I shook my head. "I'm not sure. Neither one of them is torn up about Mike's death, but both of them had significant dealings with Mike."

"Yeah, I'd say that that's why they're not torn up about Mike."

"And check this out." I pulled out my phone and brought up the pictures I'd taken of Betty's scheduling book for the Monday that Mike was killed. I zoomed the image in so that it would be easier to read and handed it over to Zoey. "Don't you think it's awfully convenient that Betty's two hairdressers are suddenly out of town and unavailable to be interviewed? There's now no one to corroborate her alibi. And, look at that. The other two hairdressers had appointment after appointment of haircuts, but look at Betty. She's got a three and a half hours blocked off for a perm. Nothing else is scheduled while the perm is setting. She could have put all those chemicals on her customer's hair and then left while the perm set. Heck, for all we know one of the other hairdressers rinsed the perm off, which would have given Betty even more time."

Zoey studied the picture. "The timing is right for Mike's death."

"And Betty saw Susie and Mike get into a big fight earlier that morning. She knew she had someone to pin it on."

"So what will going and talking to Clara in the middle of the night do for us?"

I shrugged and slouched in my seat. "We'd get the chance to really annoy her and cross her off our list of suspects?"

"Or we'd get to rattle her by showing up at her house in the middle of the night and get a confession out of her about what she really knows, 'cause she does know something. That coffee she brought over for Betty when we were talking to her was really well timed."

I was feeling happier and happier. "We gonna do this?"

"Let's do it."

Zoey put on her coat, and we collected our dishes and took them to the kitchen. Patty was clearly in her element. She was calm and focused, and she was working the red velvet cake cookie batter like it was second nature to her. All of her ingredients were measured out, and there was a tray of white goo sitting off to the side.

"What is that?" I asked.

"Marshmallows," Patty said.

"Marshmallows? You made your own?" I was in awe.

Patty looked shocked. "How else would I do it?"

I was too happy for words. I was going to be serving customers cookies with homemade marshmallow in them! I had served so many cookies, cakes and other sweets bought straight from the store. Patty's homemade marshmallows made me feel as though a new culinary level had been reached by my little café.

"We're going out," Zoey told Patty. "We'll be gone maybe an hour. You okay with that?"

"Sure," Patty said, and I believed her. She never once paused in her work. She was at home inside this kitchen. She was at peace, and she was confident.

"Thanks, Patty," I said, as Zoey shoved my coat into my arms and pulled me out the café's back door.

"She's making homemade marshmallows," I said to Zoey as soon as we got outside. "Homemade!"

"Yeah."

A noise to our left drew our attention, and we turned as one to see someone halfway up my fire escape.

"Looks like we don't have to go anywhere after all," Zoey said.

The person on the fire escape twisted around, revealing their face.

"Clara!" I said, the happiest I had been so far that night. I really, really, really needed to do some soul-searching about that. I turned to Zoey to gloat. "It's Clara."

"I—" That was all Zoey got the chance to say before ending up sprawled on the ground. Unconscious.

CHAPTER 31

"Zoey!" I reached for her, bending over, and felt the glancing blow of something unimaginably hard against the back of my head. I fell to my knees.

Another blow whizzed toward me, but I ducked my head and took the blow on my shoulder. Standing up, I staggered to the side and threw my back against the café's back door. Finally, I was able to look my would-be killer in the eyes.

"Betty!" She was standing a few feet away wielding a crowbar like a baseball bat. "I knew it!" Okay, that probably wasn't the best thing for me to say at that moment, and gloating wasn't helping, but

I had been so sure that she was the one who had killed Mike.

But Clara's presence surprised me. A part of me had really wanted her to be the killer, so I had discounted my suspicions about her, dismissing them as jealousy-driven. I wished that I'd trusted my intuition a little bit more. "When did the two of you start working together?"

Clara hopped down from the fire escape ladder. "After she went snooping through Mike's personal emails. It was allll in his emails. The dummy contract he was going to trick me with, and the fact that he was about to dump Betty and triple her rent."

"Shut up, Clara. This is all your fault."

"My fault?" Clara screeched. "Killing Mike was your idea!"

"No! My idea was to kill Mike and pin it on Tina, not Susie! But nooooo, you had to go off script, didn't you?"

"What was I supposed to do? She was there. She made the better patsy!"

I frantically tapped on the door at my back with my fingertips. I didn't know if it would be enough to draw Patty's attention, but I didn't want to alert Clara or Betty to my efforts. Zoey still wasn't moving. We needed the police, and we needed an ambulance.

"If you hadn't tried to frame Susie, these two imbeciles would have never gotten involved," Betty yelled, and then swung the crowbar so that it was pointing at me. "Don't think I didn't see you take a picture of my schedule book."

"What does it matter?" Clara hissed.

"How long do you think I could have kept her away from those two idiot assistants of mine? They would have told her I'd left the salon. She would have known it was me!"

Clara took a challenging step forward. "But she wouldn't have known it was me, would she?"

The two were facing off like Godzilla and… whoever the heck it was that Godzilla fought. Whoever it was, I was getting very concerned about being caught in the crossfire. But, there wasn't anything I could do about it. There was no way I could leave Zoey.

I had to keep them talking. The longer they were talking, the longer they wouldn't be killing me, Zoey, or each other, and the more likely someone would happen by and interrupt the whole situation.

"I still don't understand what happened. What was in the email to make you want to kill him?"

Clara shifted her attention toward me. "He was going to trick me into having sex with him!"

At Clara's mention of having sex with Mike, Betty's hands inched up on her bat hold of the crowbar. While Clara was looking at me, Betty's eyes were fixed on Clara.

"Betty! Betty!" I yelled. She shifted her glare from Clara to me. "What happened? What made you want to kill him? You were planning on marrying him."

"But he wasn't planning on marrying me." She shook her head. "How could I be so stupid? I wanted to marry him so much, and he never asked, but he never said no to any of my plans. He'd always pat me and give me a hug and say it 'sounds nice' or something else like that. I'd thought he was just one of those guys, you know? One of those guys who don't like to come out and tell you just how he feels."

"Yeah," Clara snarled. "Turns out you were right. It's just that how he felt for you was nothin'."

Betty took a swing at Clara, but Clara jumped back. In truth, Betty had missed her by a mile. If only was able to say the same about Zoey. Looking down at her, I saw her finger twitch, and it was the most glorious sight I'd ever seen. She was alive!

"And what about you?" Betty said. "What about you being willing to whore yourself out for lower rent? I should have let you go through with it after I found out he was planning on feeding you a dummy contract not worth the paper it was printed on."

"And let your boy have some fun with

this?" Clara motioned her hands up and down the length of her own body.

Betty took another swing, and this swing came much closer than the previous one.

"So you worked together," I said, eager to keep them both alive. Clara was preoccupying Betty, but if Clara went down, there would be nothing to keep Betty from turning her crowbar on Zoey and me. "How did you manage doing, you know, what you did?"

"I seduced him," Clara said, smug. She wasn't looking at me. She was giving all her hate to Betty. "I got him all distracted playing kissing face, keeping the shredder between us as a teaser. I even put that stupid scarf on him. Then Betty—"

"Shut up."

"—came up behind him—"

"Shut up."

"—and held his shoulders down once I turned the shredder on."

"Shut up!"

"Should have seen her. She cried like a

baby the whole time, told him how sorry she was."

Betty took another swing at Clara, and this time I was rooting for her. Clara was vile. Of course, Betty had killed the man she loved in cold blood, so the two of them were in good company with each other.

The crowbar connected with Clara's side with a dull thud and the whooshing exhale of all of her air. She went down on her knees, and Betty raised the crowbar for a killing blow.

"Wait!" I started to take a step forward only to be propelled off balance by the door behind bursting open. I fell on top of Zoey, and did my best to shield her body from whatever it was that was about to happen next.

Twisting, I witnessed the most awesome sight of my adult life. Patty was standing in the doorway. She had three forks in each hand, and each fork was topped with a huge glob of white goo—and that goo was on fire.

Patty pulled her arms back and then

let fly. Mounds of flame soared through the air. I screamed, covered my head with my arm and covered as much of Zoey as I could with my body. Clara and Betty screamed as well, then their screams turned to sounds of sheer panic.

"Get it off! Get it off!" they both screamed, and I looked up to find them both high stepping and waving their arms. Their coats were on fire! And that's when I saw it out of the corner of my eye, the flick of flame. My own coat was on fire!

A scream was only halfway up my throat when Patty's strong arms grabbed me and jerked my coat off my shoulders and threw it to the side. Then while Clara and Betty were trying to shed themselves of their own coats, Patty and I got on either side of Zoey and dragged her back inside the café.

"What was that?" I asked after we got the door slammed shut.

"Roasting marshmallows," Patty said, grinning from ear to ear.

Through the door, we could hear

Betty and Clara fighting with each other again. Their car keys were in their burning coat pockets. The sound of a police siren blared its way through the door next.

"Did you call the cops?" I asked Patty.

She nodded yes.

"What about an ambulance? Did you call an ambulance?" It wasn't me who asked that question. It was Zoey.

"Zoey! You're okay!" I pulled her into my arms.

"Hey, hey… Broken noggin here. Easy. No hugs. No hugs."

I ignored her and hugged her even more.

CHAPTER 32

Macaroons, sugar cookies, spice cookies, red velvet cake cookies, pecan sandies, molasses crisps, gingersnap cookies, butter cookies, snickerdoodles, oatmeal raisin and a half dozen other types of cookies lined every available inch of the grill's serving counter. Mixed in among them were an assortment of cupcakes, including carrot cake, mocha chocolate chip, banana bread, and German chocolate.

Today was open house, customer appreciation day and the cookies and drinks were free! It was an unseasonably bright, sunny day, and the café's front door stood wide open. An A-sign was set up outside letting all passersby know to come inside and enjoy. Joel had even run an ad in his paper at a steep discount (aka free), and boy had it worked. The café was teeming with customers! And to my utter shock and surprise, people weren't just getting their fill of the freebies and leaving. No, they were ordering food. Full priced food. Patty had warned me to be sure to have plenty of buy-ables on hand because I'd be making a bunch of sales, but I hadn't believed her. I was glad that I'd done as she'd said on blind faith.

While I loved the amazing feedback I was getting about all of the delicious cookies and other baked goods, I was a little sad that Patty wasn't with me. I'd tried to get her to come out with me to greet customers. I'd been eager to showcase her for her talents, but she'd quietly and politely declined and had left by the café's back entrance when the cooking was done.

That was okay. She was doing what made her happy and helped her to feel good, and that's all that really mattered.

And better still, Joel had helped Patty find a home. She was now "renting" a room from his great-aunt, Aunt Bella. Aunt Bella was an elderly lady, widowed and living alone with no children of her own. Joel said she'd been tickled pink at the idea of sharing her home. As for the rent, it consisted of companionship and a few home-cooked meals. Patty had cried tears of joy after meeting Aunt Bella and being made to feel so welcome. Her new bedroom was light, airy and full of lovely antiques. And Aunt Bella was over the moon when she learned from Patty that Patty knew how to quilt by hand. The two promised to take on a project together.

"You got any horseradish for this thing?" Zoey asked, waving a roast beef sandwich on sourdough bread at me. It was one of the buy-ables that I was offering today. I had all the sandwich parts prepped, making them super fast to throw together.

"Horseradish?" I was mortified. I didn't have any horseradish sauce. I looked around at everybody else who had bought a roast beef sandwich from me, wondering if they were missing it, too. I didn't know what it was about not having the food that was going to make people happy, but it made me feel downright awful. "I never even thought about. I didn't know people did that."

Zoey put one hand on my shoulder and gave me a wink. "It's okay. Breathe. But next time, horseradish sauce."

I looked past her, over to where Agatha and Conrad sat at a table next to one of the large windows. "It's nice of you to treat them to lunch."

Zoey shrugged. "When you're wrong, you're wrong."

"What convinced you that Conrad was an okay guy?"

"I called up and talked to his first wife. He married very soon after their divorce. I figured if anyone would be willing to dish dirt on him, it'd be her."

"What happened?"

Zoey shook her head like she still couldn't believe it. "She raved about him.

Couldn't get a bad word out of her. She'd wanted the divorce. He insisted his lawyer be fair in splitting their assets. During the divorce, he fell in love with his attorney's assistant and married her, and he stayed devoted to her until her death." She shrugged again. "And that's it. No dirt. No underhanded dealings. Nothing."

Zoey headed back to their table, and I gazed wistfully at Agatha. She was radiant in her happiness. If a much younger, successful man were interested in me, I'd worry myself into misery about our differences. I'd let all my insecurities ruin what was good. But not Agatha. I had so much to learn from that wonderful woman.

But Zoey was no slouch either, even with her contrasting distrust of men and generally surly disposition. She was as resilient as a volcano. After being hit on the head, she'd bounced back quickly. She'd nursed a massive headache for about three days, but she was now back to her old self. In fact, I wasn't sure but I think she might have been hired to hack a bank trustee's records in Zurich in search of unreported war artifacts. All I know is that I'd overheard several snippets of conversation that had been very interesting.

As for the rest of my regulars, they were tucked away in the cozy corner. I wasn't sure they were enjoying my customer appreciation day as much as I was. They'd been pushed aside while every Tom, Dick and Harry found their way off the street to check out what the café had to offer. But it was worth it. My earnings from today were looking like they would put a good dent in what I owed on the new boiler, which was now thankfully installed and operational.

"Could I order an assortment of four dozen cookies for pickup two weeks from now?" a woman asked as people meandered around her, picking this or that cookie to take with them back to their tables.

"Uh… Um…" A cold sweat broke out on my upper lip. Patty had made every single one of the cookies on display. She'd given me the recipes, but I was nowhere near being able to pull them off. I'd tried to make the sugar cookies, but they'd tasted like bland cornbread. "I… sure. Yes. I can do that." My cold sweat migrated to my forehead. Either Patty was going to help me fill that order, or I was going to have a lot of late, late nights practicing her recipes.

"Great!" the woman said.

"Oh! We can order these?" a man next to her asked with more excitement than I was comfortable with. "I want a dozen and a half of the red velvet cupcakes and a dozen and a half of the German Chocolate cupcakes."

I opened my mouth but only a squeak came out, and my cold sweat was well on its way to turning into a full body-drenching flop sweat. "I… We…" I swallowed hard. "When do you need them?"

"Day after tomorrow," the man said. "I can pay for them now." He already had his credit card in his hand, and he hadn't even bothered to ask how much the cupcakes would be.

I was in over my head.

I was in over my head with success.

Oh my… My biggest challenge yet!

JOIN THE A.R. WINTERS NEWSLETTER

Find out about the latest releases by AR Winters, and get access to exclusive free copies of her books:

CLICK HERE TO JOIN

You can also follow AR Winters on Facebook

Made in United States
Orlando, FL
12 November 2024

53807732R10257